SHAKING UP THE HOUSE

SHAKING UP THE HOUSE

Yamile Saied Méndez

HARPER
An Imprint of HarperCollins*Publishers*

For Brielle Black, my niece, with all my love

SHAKING UP THE HOUSE

WINNIE

Winnie didn't think it all the way through.

Typical Winnie.

But to be fair, this morning there was no one around to tell her not to do it, for once. A legit miracle in this house that was always teeming with people busy like ants at a picnic. Besides, the floors were freshly waxed, and, best of all, she was wearing soft, fluffy socks.

Perfect combination.

All the canned energy of having to act properly through another photo op made her skin crawl. And since she couldn't hide at Blair House, what better way to release the tension than a mini-adventure on her way to the North Lawn?

1

The first time her family had received the official White House Christmas tree, she'd been so excited she'd cried. She'd also only been four. Eight years of the same thing later (standing in the cold, smiling at the cameras, and putting on her Perfect First Daughter face), the excitement of another holiday season under the spotlight had lost its shine. Still, she had to do what she had to do. She tucked her shoes against the wall, out of her path.

A quick glance over her shoulder confirmed that no Secret Service agents were camouflaged against the flowery wallpaper or behind a curtain in the Solarium.

Faintly, she remembered Mami's words from the other day: *"Winnie, why are you always listening to the voice of mischief instead of the voice of reason? You need to set a good example!"*

Even now she didn't have an answer. Instead, she laughed and broke into a run to get momentum.

With a wild "Woo-hoo," she pushed off the banister and slid down down the ramp.

She closed her eyes, as if that could quiet the critical voices in her head and vanish the judgy eyes watching her from the portraits on the wall. Never in a million years would they have imagined a dark-skinned Latina girl as one of America's first daughters. She wasn't going to miss them or this house. She'd never say so out loud, though. If people knew her true feelings, they would call her spoiled, entitled, ungrateful.

The executive mansion, the president's palace, the People's House (as Papi called it) . . . the White House featured a hundred and thirty-five rooms, a florist, a chocolatier, a bowling alley, a private theater, and a million other perks. What else could a kid want?

But people didn't understand. Who'd want to grow up in a museum?

And that's what the house ultimately was: a museum. Winnie felt like of the pandas at the National Zoo, always under the spotlight. She was grateful about all the comforts, and especially the chocolate lava cake Chef Jean-Paul made when Winnie had a particularly bad day. But with the perks came the pitfalls.

She couldn't even open a window without creating a scene or ruining the vacations of innocent tourists who'd only wanted a glimpse of one of the most iconic residences in the world.

Winnie hadn't seen photos of the new house in California yet, but Tía Suz had assured her it had floor-to-ceiling windows to take advantage of the golden sunshine in the afternoons, and the sounds of singing birds and the waves of the ocean. Winnie was holding on to that promise. She couldn't wait to leave the White House forever.

All these thoughts blurred through her mind in the five seconds her adventure lasted.

Next thing she knew, she had crashed head-on into

someone. Winnie bounced back and landed on her bottom.

"What in the world?" the other person exclaimed.

The other person was none other than Paloma López, J.D., *the* first lady of the United States (FLOTUS for short), code name Pinnacle. In other words, her mom.

Mami.

Of all the people coming and going through this house, it had to be her! Winnie would never *not* be grounded.

Somehow, her mom had managed not to fall with the force of the impact. Still, she placed a hand on the wall, as if she needed to steady herself at the sight of her older daughter, the rambunctious one. As usual, Mami looked immaculate in a snow-white coat, dark wool slacks, and black boots with three-inch heels. Her dark skin gleamed, flawless, thanks to excellent genes and the meticulous nighttime skin-care routine Winnie had never had the patience to imitate. Her black hair was arranged in a tight ballerina bun at the base of her neck. But Mami's delicate features were deceiving. Under the elegance, there was solid granite.

"Ow." Winnie rubbed her forehead.

"Winifred Esperanza López Bianchi," Mami said in that voice that cut through ice, diamonds, and flitting fantasies of adventure. "What in the world were you thinking, young lady? The carriage is almost here! We've all been looking for you, and here you are, acting like a kindergartner instead of a señorita of twelve. No, I take that back. When you were a kindergartner, you had better manners. Pero niña!"

Full name *and* Spanglish? Winnie was in serious trouble.

She decided to appeal to her mom's tender feelings. Paloma had been trying to act composed for the press, the staff, and Winnie's dad, who had so much to do in his last weeks as the president of the United States they hardly ever saw him. But Winnie knew Mami's emotions had been all over the place. Moving out after such a long time was wreaking havoc on the whole family.

Gingerly, Winnie clambered back to her feet and lowered her head. "I'm sorry, Mami. I promise it won't happen again."

Paloma laughed. A short, high-pitched yap that unsettled Winnie more than if her mom had sent her to her room. "Ay, mi amor! If I had a penny for every time you've said you were sorry and you promised not to do it again, I'd've been able to fund my reading program the first year of Papi's presidency."

Tentatively, Winnie walked toward Mami, and in a somber voice that couldn't really hide the excitement, said, "In less than seven weeks, I won't even be able to do this anymore."

"Counting down the days, are you?"

"And the hours."

Her mom laughed for real this time and brushed a hand over Winnie's head, then glanced back at the polished wood access ramp. "I'm sure that when FDR had this installed, he never imagined it would double as a ski-jumping platform."

Encouraged by the tender expression in Mami's eyes, Winnie said, "You see an access ramp, I see an *American Ninja Warrior* inverted warp wall. . . ."

Mami looked puzzled.

"That floor-obstacle thingie they have on the show," Winnie explained.

"Oh, mi amor. You and your imagination."

Since the Olympics were kind of impossible, Winnie dreamed of putting her gymnastic skills to good use in a proper obstacle course. For some weird reason though, Papi had never agreed to build her one. *That* would have been an epic legacy to leave behind for future first children.

Paloma shook her head, but when she looked down at Winnie, her eyes widened in alarm.

"What happened to your sweater? It's torn."

With dread, Winnie inspected the sleeve of her cotton-candy-pink pullover. A tear ran from the elbow to the wrist. "Oh no," she said.

For weeks, she and Ingrid, her eleven-year-old sister, had looked at catalogs and websites trying to find the perfect outfits for today and all the events coming up during the busy holiday season. Ingrid wasn't a fashionista like their mom, but she cared a lot about her looks. They helped her get in character for each occasion, she usually said. Winnie only played along with her planning to make sure the clothes they chose allowed for freedom of movement, aka jumps and back handsprings. And now all the months of negotiation had gone down the trash, because there was no way Winnie could go out and receive the Christmas tree in a holey sweater.

"I'm so sorry, Mami . . . but look, I can keep my arm stuck to my body like this," she said, demonstrating, walking like a member of the Old Guard. "No one will notice, I swear. I'll change into something else as soon as we come back into the house."

Her mom wasn't smiling now. "Hija, remember. Not only do you represent our family, you're the face of our country. More importantly, our Latin community and our culture. From all sides of the political spectrum, people look up to us as either good examples to follow or terrible ones to avoid."

"Examples to destroy, you mean," Winnie muttered, and then she asked, "What about those talks about being myself, and following my heart—"

"With great privilege comes a lot of power and also responsibility. By the way, there's a bundle of letters ready for you to read and reply to."

Winnie stifled a groan. She loved some of the letters she got from people all over the world. She especially liked the ones she got from kids her own age whose lives were so different from hers. The staff curated the letters, but once a terrible postcard criticizing Winnie for how loud she'd laughed in a TV interview had somehow missed the purge and gotten to her hands. She'd tried to forget the worst parts, but the phrase "You're not good enough to be in the White House" in Spanish had never really left her.

The pressure to be perfect was too much. What Mami said was true. But why was she responsible for representing the whole of Latin culture? Her parents were of Mexican and Argentine heritage, two countries that were big, unique, and diverse, but for some reason she was supposed to match both perfectly. Not only that, but also she needed to fit the ideal image of a young Latina for all of Latin America and the US. It was impossible!

Winnie didn't get to complain, though. Her mom was gently leading her forward into action. "Vamos, change the face. And pick up your shoes."

Winnie dragged her feet in the hallway. From the corner of her eye, she saw one of the butlers, Weston, changing a flower vase. He must have heard the whole argument. She should have gotten used to people seeing her in every circumstance, but she never had, and now it was too late. She wished she could pull a preteen-rage card and slam a door, but she could never. She was brash and impulsive, but she cared about her family and respected the staff too much to make them uncomfortable.

Mami urged her, "Please, run to your room and change. Alice made sure we ordered two sweaters in case something like this happened."

Alice Sung was Mami's chief of staff, and she had saved Winnie more times than she could count.

One of Mami's phones chimed with an incoming message, and she glanced down at it. "I'll come along so you don't get lost on any other adventures," she said. "We only have five minutes and we can't be late."

That her mom personally had to escort her to make sure she didn't destroy herself or anything else was a new low.

A heavy feeling settled on Winnie, her own personal gray cloud that she didn't know how to shake off.

Maybe Mami could feel its hold on Winnie, because she said, "Why don't you invite a friend to come over tomorrow?" Her voice was chirpy but also careful, like she was trying to find the best words to make Winnie feel better. "You've been talking about this new girl at school. What's her name? Anjali?"

For a second Winnie got excited, but realizing all the hoops Anjali would have to go through just for a sleepover at the White House, she knew it wasn't worth it. "No, thanks. Nothing like telling a prospective new friend they need to have a full background check extending five generations back to kill the vibe."

"And why don't you go to her house?"

Now it was time for Winnie to laugh sarcastically. Picturing Agent Sisco or one of the other agents snuggled in a sleeping bag in Anjali's living room, all because Winnie wanted a sleepover, made her shiver. Been there, done that. No, thanks.

"No, Mami. Besides, didn't you say we needed to simplify our already hectic life?"

"See? You do listen to what I say after all," Paloma said, walking into Winnie's room.

Winnie turned on the light and smiled at the sight of the extra pink sweater on her bed. She made a mental note to thank Alice for her ability to see the future.

She took off the torn one, put on the new one, and turned to face her mom.

Paloma was in inspecting mode, and after a brief nod of approval at Winnie's appearance, her eyes continued sweeping through the room. Before her mom started pointing out imperfections, Winnie said, "I promise I'll clean Lafayette's cage tomorrow. I haven't had the chance yet."

"You needed to finish *all* your chores yesterday, Win. Not just the ones you felt like doing."

"I don't understand why the staff can't help me when I'm swamped with homework, Mami." She didn't say how she was hardly keeping up. She didn't want to get in any more trouble.

Her mom pinched her nose with her fingers and in a nasal voice said, "You're the one who insisted on taking care of this ferret yourself. How you can sleep with this odiferous beast in your room is beyond me. How you and your father convinced me to get you a ferret is a mystery. Why couldn't you choose something sensible, like a labradoodle?"

As if he'd known they were talking about him, First Ferret Lafayette, Laffy for short, peeked his pointy face from his sleeping hammock. With a swift turn of his body, he was sniffing between the cage's thin bars, making dooking sounds of happiness like he was giggling.

Winnie fed him one of his favorite turkey treats. "Labradoodles are predictable."

Her mom scoffed, and Winnie added, "At least it's not an alligator like President Adams's, or a raccoon like President Coolidge's!"

Paloma laughed, covering her mouth with a perfectly manicured hand.

"It's true! He named her Rebecca. Imagine a raccoon with the same name as Abuela," Winnie said.

Winnie wasn't the comedian of the family—that would

be Ingrid—but she did love making her mom laugh. Especially after getting into so much trouble on a Saturday morning.

"Let's go, Popcorn," Mami said, using the code name the Secret Service had given Winnie. It had sounded cute years ago, but now it made her cringe.

"Kettle corn or butter?" Winnie asked.

Mami smiled. "Both! Now, come on. It's the *pinnacle* of impoliteness to make people wait for you." Then she added, "Like you said, a few more weeks, and this is all over."

She sounded sad, but to Winnie, Inauguration Day was the light at the end of a tunnel that in the last few months had gotten darker and darker.

After a childhood under the public's eye, she was ready for a normal sleepover with friends. For not having to explain the surveillance closet in a hall at school to new students. She couldn't wait to be a normal twelve-year-old, free to run wild in the house, slide on the floor with her fluffy socks, or open a window to let out the smell of her pet's rancid cage and let in crisp wintery air.

INGRID

Although it was still early, the White House entrance was already bustling with activity. Just the way Ingrid liked her mornings—whirlwind-y. She smiled and waved at the tourists huddled by the fence along the North Lawn. If it weren't for the frigid air, she would sit outside and talk to people all day.

"I can't imagine not being here next year," she said to Sally, one of the holiday volunteer coordinators. Sally was old enough to be her grandma, but Ingrid loved her as a friend. "I just can't."

Sally pouted. "And I can't imagine this place without you. The first time you were—what?—three, four years old?"

"Three!" Ingrid said, waving at the dozens of volunteers

coming off a bus. Every December, they arrived to decorate the most famous house in the country.

Ingrid wouldn't be here when they came back to take things down. Now she was the one pouting.

Sally one-arm-hugged her. "We need to make the most of it, then. It's the last one, but it will be the *best* time."

"Mami said this season's plans blew her socks off."

Poor Sally had just sipped from her coffee cup. She swallowed quickly but still choked with laughter.

Ingrid patted her back. "There, there."

When Sally could speak again, she shook her head at Ingrid and said, "Ingrid, you and your wittiness. I could never picture your mom using those words."

Ingrid wrinkled her nose. "Well, she has used the words 'season plans' and 'socks' plenty of times. Not in that combination, but I promise she looked excited, like her socks were really blown off."

Sally laughed again as she headed toward the line of volunteers.

With the help of the fleet of decorators and Ingrid's stream of jokes, the White House already felt festive and warm like the woolen blankets Abuelita Leti, Papi's mom, knitted for the whole family. The only missing piece was the main tree that would lord it over them all in the Blue Room, and which was rolling in on a carriage *right now.*

Where were Mami, Papi, and Winnie?

Ingrid looked over her shoulder into the house.

"Good morning, Ingrid," Chief of Staff Alice Sung said on her way to talk to the reporters waiting beyond a barricade. "Ready for today?"

Ingrid struck the Megan Rapinoe pose. "Always! It's showtime, baby!"

Alice laughed, and a rush of victory went to Ingrid's head. She was the only one who could make the sternest woman in the White House laugh like this.

"I like your scarf! Fancy!" Ingrid called.

"Thanks for recommending it!" said the chief of staff, waving her hand back at Ingrid. The turquoise scarf was the only pop of color in Alice's wardrobe of different shades of black.

"I have more recommendations in my notebook!" Ingrid replied, taking her Book of Risas out of her parka pocket. But Alice was already gone.

A couple of minutes later, Ingrid was still making notes in the book where she wrote her practice jokes when Mami and Winnie arrived. They looked so alike, from the dark shade of their skin to their stony expressions. Ingrid took after Papi, tall and lanky, with the same cowlick in the center of their heads, making their hair stick out in all directions.

The horses' hooves clackety-clacked on the pavers, and the smell of pine, combined with that of hay and horses, made Ingrid's nose tickle.

Ingrid covered her sneeze with her elbow and whispered, "You're late."

Winnie sent her a Grinch-y look before going back to staring ahead. Ingrid followed her sister's gaze across the North Lawn, the security barrier, the naked trees at the corner of Pennsylvania Avenue and Jackson Place, kitty-corner from the White House's entrance.

All she could see was the remodeling vans parked in front of Blair House—the president's guest house and Winnie's hiding place when things became too much at the White House.

"Were you at Blair's?" Ingrid asked, hurt her sister hadn't invited her to come along.

Winnie scowled. "I can't now, can I? Papi said it's out of bounds forever!"

Ingrid looked at their mom. "But it was supposed to be ready this week."

Mami sighed and scratched the back of her head like she always did when she was stressed. "There're always complications in this kind of historical building. But this is horrible timing for another pipe to burst. We needed that house fully operational by tomorrow."

"At least this time it wasn't your fault, Winnie," Ingrid said. "Remember when you made popcorn and accidentally set the timer for eleven minutes instead of one minute and ten seconds, and the microwave had to be replaced and Blair House smelled like burned popcorn for months?"

Winnie flinched. "Why did you remind me of that now when Mami just forgave me?"

"Ay, Win, I said this water pipe destruction thing at least *wasn't* your fault!" Ingrid muttered. "I was just trying to cheer you up."

"Stop it," Winnie snarled. "It's not working."

"Chicas," Mami whispered in a warning tone while still smiling. "Please don't start a fight in front of the press. What did Papi say?"

"A better question is, where is Papi?" Ingrid replied.

Mami sighed. "Something urgent came up," she said. "He'll meet us inside in a few minutes. Now smile, Winnie, please."

Ingrid saw that her sister was trying and failing to look happy, so she knew she had to compensate, even if Papi's absence had put a damper on the whole thing.

Luckily, the horses were here.

"What's that on your head, little pony?" she exclaimed, and darted toward the giant black Clydesdale horses pulling the carriage. She jumped, trying to touch the white feather, and when the horse dipped his head and bumped his nose on Ingrid's forehead, everyone ran in her direction to make sure she was okay.

"I'm fine!" she said. "I just got a little horse snot in my hair now, that's all."

After a few more seconds of this clowning around, even Winnie was smiling.

Being funny was a lot of effort, and Ingrid worked up a sweat trying to keep everyone around her happy. But at least the photo op was a success.

Later, sealed inside the house, Ingrid didn't have to worry about diverting the press attention from her sister's bad vibes. Matías López was speaking.

He had so many names. The world called him Mr. President. Ingrid and Winnie called him Papi. Mami called him Amor. The family called him Nene. (Even though he was in his late forties, he'd always be the baby to his parents and siblings.) The Secret Service had given him the code name Pioneer.

For the first of many things, the name fit him perfectly. The first American-born citizen in his family, the first college graduate, and then the first Latino president of the whole country, he'd blazed the way for generations to come.

Papi had certainly made his mark on history. He'd never be forgotten.

Now he was talking about plans for the future as the whole press corps hung on his every word. "I know the girls are excited for this new chapter in our lives." He looked at Winnie, whose eyes were glazed over like she was thousands of miles away in her mind, and continued, "Especially Susana. The other day she told me she can't wait for her share of California sun."

"Susana?" Ingrid couldn't help it. She blurted the question out loud enough for the whole room to hear. Susana was her dad's older sister, Tía Suz. When he was ultra-exhausted, her dad always mixed up names. Good thing he had Ingrid in his corner. "Someone get this man a coffee!" she exclaimed, pointing at her dad.

The whole room exploded in laughter, including her dad. Ingrid loved how the crinkles in the corners of his eyes transformed his face when he smiled. She got a glimpse of what a young Matías López had looked like when he arrived at the White House eight years ago with dreams of changing the world. Of course she couldn't remember anything from that day. She'd been too little, but she'd seen pictures and video.

Ah! She loved the way her dad smiled.

"Good one, Parakeet," Alice whispered next to her. Ingrid glared at Alice, who smiled, although the glare wasn't a joke.

Parakeet was the code name the Secret Service had

given *her* when, even as a toddler, she wouldn't stop chattering away. Abuelita Leti always said Ingrid had been born speaking both English and Spanish and a language only the family could understand, Ingridish.

Ingrid had never minded her code name before, but since last year, she wished they'd thought of a different one. A friend at school had showed her caricatures people online made of Ingrid as a parrot. Even though she'd tried to follow Papi's advice to brush the negative things off her shoulders, every time someone called her Parakeet, she felt an uncomfortable twinge.

Next to her, Winnie sighed. Bad moods were certainly catching.

As she did every time dark vibes threatened her family, Ingrid tried to diffuse them by making everyone laugh. Laughter was like magic. It could vaporize even the beginnings of a family storm.

Before she could think things through, Ingrid elbowed her sister.

"What?" Winnie asked, rubbing her arm. "What did you do that for?"

Instead of replying, Ingrid stuck her tongue out at Winnie, whose face remained stony. "You're so annoying."

"And you're always so gloomy," Ingrid whispered back. "You've been acting more like an Eeyore than a Winnie lately."

Winnie's mouth twitched, like she was repressing a smile, but she turned back to look at the window.

Ingrid gave up. In a way, she understood her sister. Ingrid couldn't imagine saying goodbye to the people she'd learned to love as family. Nancy in the florist shop, Leo and Jennifer in the Calligraphy Office, Otto, the chocolatier. Thomas, and his office of ushers, each in charge of a different aspect of running the house: housekeeping, food and beverage, flowers, and events. The maids, carpenters, engineers, and yes, even the Secret Service agents. Like she'd told Sally earlier, she couldn't imagine her life without all the people she'd seen every day at the house.

After the move, life at the house would continue the same as always, but the López family wouldn't be the First anymore.

There was no getting away from hearing about the move, though. That was all the reporters talked about, as if they were ready to close this chapter on the López administration.

Chantel, one of the reporters, asked, "Mr. President, tell us about the logistics of Inauguration Day. Your family moves out the same day President-Elect Williams's family moves in. That's a lot of moving parts."

There was a ripple of chuckles across the room, and Ingrid scoffed.

"Shhh," Mami said, placing a hand over hers.

"That wasn't even a good joke," she complained. "Besides, Inauguration Day is weeks away! Why are—"

Mami pressed Ingrid's hand and leaned over to whisper in her ear, "Papi has a surprise. Listen." She signaled with her puckered lips toward Ingrid's dad, whose face was all lit up. He loved surprises.

Ingrid sat on the edge of her seat to better hear his words.

"Yes, like you said, there are so many moving parts. The wizards who make it happen seamlessly are already hard at work planning every detail," Papi said in his casual president voice.

Carlos Rojas, one of Ingrid's favorite correspondents, asked, "Will your girls and President-Elect Williams's daughters get to spend some time together before your family heads to California? They got to know each other during the campaign, right?"

"Yes, the four of them are good friends," the president said. "This is why I'm sure my announcement will be a great holiday present for my daughters."

Every eye turned toward Winnie and Ingrid.

Winnie kept looking at the window like a trapped bird dreaming of flying away.

But at the mention of presents and the Williams sisters, Ingrid jumped to her feet and clapped.

"I love you, Zora and Skylar!" she exclaimed, blowing a kiss to one of the cameras.

During the campaign, she and Winnie had totally clicked with Zora and Skylar Williams, twelve-year-old twins, identical in every way but their personalities. Maybe it was that the four girls understood each other like no one else ever could. After all, the First Kids Club was a very exclusive group that no one was really prepared to join. Ingrid couldn't wait to welcome the Williams sisters to it.

After another bout of laughter rippled through the room, the president continued talking. "It's tradition for the president-elect and their family to move into Blair House after the election."

From the corner of her eye, Ingrid noticed that at the mention of Blair House, Winnie's spine had stiffened, her attention fully on Papi's next words.

"But what about the remodeling going on at Blair House after the pipe burst?" one of the reporters asked, voicing Ingrid's questions. "Is it finished?"

The president's eyes glinted. "The *restoration* of Blair House, like most restoration jobs, is taking a *little* longer than expected." He glanced at Mami and grimaced almost imperceptibly.

Mami shook her head and pressed her lips as if trying not to smile.

"Beau Williams had mentioned he wanted the twins to be established in the area well before January 20," Carlos continued. "Since Blair House is unavailable, will the future first family stay at a nearby hotel?"

The president took a big breath and said, "Paloma and Mr. Williams have been communicating daily about this dilemma. As you know, Carlos, school resumes at the beginning of January, and moving into a new house while trying to keep up with school isn't the best situation. So my wife and I had an idea. . . ."

Mami pressed Ingrid's hand. "Here it is. Listen."

"The holiday season is a time for traditions, family, hospitality, and friendship. The arrival of my family in the White House gave rise to a lot of new traditions. Some were received better than others . . . ," he said, and a mixture of laughter and embarrassed looks passed through the room. "Considering we have more than one hundred and thirty rooms in this house, we'd like to extend our hospitality to the Williams family and share the house with them," the president continued. "That is, until Inauguration Day, when my family moves out, and the Williamses officially move into the executive residence. I think it's a wonderful plan."

A buzz went across the room.

"Really, Mami?" Ingrid asked. "I've always wanted to be one of the official tour guides! I promise I'll make sure Zora and Skylar are ready for the best years of their lives!"

Mami laughed. "Shhh. He's not done."

The president kept talking about the logistics of sharing

the house with the Williamses, but Ingrid was too excited to pay attention to his words. She was already miles ahead, planning to show Zora and Skylar the Lincoln Bedroom, the Queens' Bedroom, the chocolate replica of the White House, and all the nooks and crannies that no "Secrets of the White House" YouTube video included.

Having two friends her age living at the home where she'd been so happy was a dream.

WINNIE

After the grand announcement and the obligatory photo op, Winnie ran up to the residence to grab her phone and text Skylar and Zora.

Ingrid chased after her, climbing the stairs two at a time. "Wait for me, Win!"

Winnie couldn't contain herself, but when she took her phone from the cabinet in the kitchen, she paused for a second. She needed to catch her breath anyway.

"What are you doing?" Ingrid asked.

The kitchen and family area room were filling up with people.

"What does it look like I'm doing? Why haven't they texted me already?" Winnie said while she typed, *I can't believe it! We're so excited!*

But the minutes passed, and the twins didn't reply.

"Maybe they got their phones taken away?" Ingrid said. "Remember what a hassle it was for us to finally get phones?"

Winnie remembered, and she suppressed a shudder. Poor Zora and Skylar. Their lives were about to change drastically.

"Chicas," Mami called from the other side of the family room. "Please finish your homework for Monday, because tomorrow's a big day."

An army of aides and attendants already milled around them, finishing the last-minute details before the big move.

"Can we go to my room?" Winnie asked, but Ingrid was shaking her head. "I don't want to go to your room, Win! This is too exciting!"

"How are we supposed to do any homework here?" Winnie muttered.

A young aide looked in their direction, and Winnie angled her body to talk to her sister without anyone eavesdropping.

They had zero privacy, but through trial and error, Winnie and Ingrid had perfected their secret-sharing system. Not that they'd ever had anything super exciting to hide from the Secret Service and other White House staff, but it was annoying when rumors of their latest crushes spread around the staff.

"I wonder why Mami and Papi wouldn't tell us before announcing it to the whole world," Winnie said, voicing the thought that had nagged at her since the press conference.

"It was a surprise," Ingrid said, scratching her head. "It makes sense. . . ."

"Not really." Winnie shrugged one shoulder. "I'd have liked a little more time to prepare a welcome for Sky and Zora."

"I know!" Ingrid replied. "Like those welcome practical jokes the staff plays on each other."

"Practical jokes?"

Before she replied, Ingrid glanced up at Mami, who had a radar for detecting troublemaking. But why would she look at them with so much suspicion? This time they hadn't even started *planning* trouble.

But before Winnie could look guilty in advance, Mami's phone rang.

"No. Not satin," she said. "Theresa's assistant said she prefers one-hundred-percent pima cotton. Cream. Please make the room look and feel homier than a hotel."

Next to her, Alice gave instructions to the head housekeepers. "Make sure the girls' favorite treats are all stocked: Nutella sticks and red grapes. Ah, one more thing. I know it will be hard, but do try not to call the twins by each other's name. They're identical, but Zora's a little shy, and Skylar loves fashion. She usually wears a bow or another kind of cute hair accessory."

"Does President-Elect Williams prefer coffee or tea?" Nelson, the head butler, asked.

Alice didn't even check her clipboard to reply, "Coffee." And then, answering the silent questions on his face, she added, "Colombian. French press. No sugar. A splash of half-and-half."

The woman was a human computer.

But someone was missing from the crowd of staff. Winnie looked around, but Agent Sisco was nowhere to be seen.

Before Winnie could ask her sister to expand on those practical jokes she'd been talking about, Ingrid leaned in closer and whispered, "The next few weeks are going to be epic. I'll get to give them a tour and show them all over the house. The other day, Mami said that they'll attend a different school from ours. Bummer, because wouldn't it be fun to ride with them every day? But, oh well . . . I always wished there were more of us, you know? Siblings, I mean. Imagine all the fun we'll have with them! Those few days in the campaign were a blast. Last week when I asked Papi about hanging out with the twins, he hinted at a surprise, but this beats anything I could've come up with. Picture this! If we . . ."

Ingrid went on and on for minutes. Winnie let her sister run out of steam. She knew from experience that the best way—the only way—to get a word in when Ingrid was excited was just to let her talk. And that's what she did. Typical Ingrid, wishing for more people, as if there weren't enough people milling about them. All. Day. Long.

Winnie's gaze darted to the grown-ups. Everyone was 100 percent engaged in best-hosts-ever mode.

"So the other day, when I was waiting for you to be done swimming laps in the pool, I overheard one of the clerks mention to one of the maids about a little tradition here at the house," Ingrid said. At "tradition" her eyes glinted with excitement, bringing Winnie back to the present.

Winnie wiggled her eyebrows. "Finally."

Ingrid continued, "You know the Williamses will bring their own staff and stuff to the house, right?"

Winnie narrowed her eyes. "Not really . . . the staff will remain the same."

"The president will appoint new chiefs of departments, though."

"Sure, but when I asked Nelson if they would all be fired, he said no. It would be impossible to train new people."

"Exactly," Ingrid said. "And some of them, like Nelson, have been here for decades—"

"Keep it down, Ingrid," Winnie said, alarmed at how the volume of her sister's voice kept increasing.

Ingrid hunched her shoulders and continued whispering. "The new president will bring in her own chief of staff and people. Even some Secret Service officers will be new. Sisco is retiring. But I'm talking about the administrative staff. On Inauguration Day, everything will be switched from the López administration to the Williams one in the space of a few hours. Did you not pay attention to Papi's reminder of what the process is like at the press conference?"

"Ingridcita, I heard every word. I just can't wait to be free once and for all."

"Free? We'll be gone and forgotten," Ingrid said in a whiny voice. "I mean, don't get me wrong, I'm thrilled Zora and Sky will be here tomorrow. But now nothing will ever be the same."

"Two administrations," Winnie said, barely able to hide her excitement. "So many people. It'll be chaos."

Ingrid leaned forward, clutching that journal, her Book of Risas, close to her heart.

"Well, if we follow along this tradition I was telling you about, it'll also be fun. Listen, did you know that when the Clintons moved out so George W. Bush could move in, the staff removed all the Ws from all the keyboards?"

Winnie had heard even worse things. "They removed

some of the doorknobs, so people would be locked in different rooms, and glued desk and dresser drawers shut!"

Ingrid shook her head and clicked her tongue, just like Mami did when she disapproved of something. "Imagine how much money it would cost to replace those antique doorknobs. And there have to be about three million keyboards. Imagine having to replace all those! And gluing the drawers? What would Mami say if we ever did something like that?"

"If she gets furious when we leave candy wrappers in the car," Winnie said, "what would she say if we leave a trace of destruction behind us? Remember, we have to appear perfect for the public. All those pranks sound more like vandalism to me. That's just being mean."

She was reckless, but not destructive.

Ingrid placed a hand over Winnie's. "I know! Those were just examples," Ingrid said. "This time, the clerks might hide the staplers or something like that, silly!"

"What does that have to do with Sky and Zora?" Winnie asked.

Ingrid smiled like a cat. "I thought it would be fun to play some kind of practical joke on the Williams twins. But more like a welcome than a prank."

Butterflies tickled Winnie's stomach. She loved the idea, but what had Mami said about her never listening to the voice of reason?

"We can't go overboard, though, right?"

"Never!" Ingrid said, raising her hand as if she were taking an oath. "But remember, nothing we do will ever be considered as going overboard. This house has seen way more first-children mischief than we could ever come up with. Come on, Winnie. You used to be fun."

Something prickled at Winnie's heart. "I am fun, Ingrid. . . . It's just that Mami always says we're being judged just by living here. I promised her I'd be a little more thoughtful."

"And what better way to be thoughtful!" Ingrid exclaimed. When Alice turned to look at her, she dropped her voice to a whisper. "You know? It's not like we're Tad Lincoln—"

"Bratty Tad, you mean?" Winnie said with a smirk.

Once, when Mami had complained about her behavior, Winnie had brought up Lincoln's youngest son's shenanigans in the White House. Mami had cut her off real quick, but she hadn't forgotten.

"We're talking about President Lincoln's son here. Winnie, be serious, please," Ingrid said, imitating Mami's tone of voice, but her eyes were shiny like she was talking about a hero.

Winnie shrugged. "He only got away with his antics because his ancestors didn't have our melanin." She pursed her lips and shook her head. "If we did a tenth of what he did, we'd be grounded until our thirties."

"He really was the king of pranks," Ingrid continued. "He hitched goats to a chair and went through the East Wing like it was a sled."

Winnie rolled her eyes but she still smiled. "Goats?"

"Yes, goats! He named them Nannie and Nanko. Cute, huh? He also had two ponies. In the White House!"

"If only Mami would let us get ponies. She doesn't even let me ride horses after I fell that one time."

"Well, you jumped when the instructor said not to. I mean, it was hilarious to see you flailing in the air, but still."

Winnie pretended to be offended. "Ay! I could've died!"

Ingrid shook her head. "Tad was a brat *and* a tyrant," Ingrid said, "but he also was the one who started the turkey pardon tradition. Papi told me."

Winnie felt a warmth bloom in her chest for poor Tad, who'd died way too young. She always had a soft spot for another fellow animal lover.

"And here we are," Winnie said. "Talking about Tad a century and a half later. An iconic first child if there ever was one. Through the stories of his pranks, it's like he never left the White House after all."

Her words made the air between the sisters buzz with electricity.

"Winnie," Ingrid said, a mischievous glint in her eye. "I

believe the guardian angel of first daughters is trying to tell us we must make the best of this situation. This is the first time ever that two administrations will share the house."

Winnie twirled a thread from her pink sweater between her fingers. "We wouldn't trash the rooms or destroy *any* property, right?"

"Of course not! But imagine the stories people will tell about us," Ingrid said, her eyes looking into the distance as if she could see the future. "One day, they might even make movies about our adventures. At the very least, a documentary or something. Seven weeks. One house. Two families. Four first daughters. Who will be the most beloved and remembered?"

"Not that the pranking will go on for seven weeks, Ingrid. A little welcome joke will be enough," Winnie said, her brain straining to find an idea. "Nothing too extreme. . . ."

Someone dropped a platter with finger foods, startling the girls and sending people scurrying all over the place.

To say things were tense around them was an understatement.

"*Everyone* in this house needs to take a chill pill, don't you think?" Winnie said. "It's the holidays, and everyone's freaking out just because of a move."

Ingrid looked at their mom, sitting in front of a computer. A map of the residential section of the house took up the whole screen. Lines of worry crisscrossed Paloma's forehead. She never got rattled, or at least never showed it, but now she definitely looked like she could use some laughter. She'd clearly known about the Williamses moving in way before Papi announced it, but that didn't mean she wasn't stressed.

As if she could sense that the girls were looking at her, Paloma turned her attention to them and smiled, shrugging a shoulder. She rose from her chair and walked toward them. Winnie was happy to have finished her math function graphs for the test coming up so she could show she'd been busy.

Paloma placed a hand on each girl's shoulder. "I'm sorry it's so loud here. Win, you're right. Maybe it would've been better for you to study somewhere else."

"The Solarium?" she asked. Maybe she could slide down the ramp with Ingrid before bedtime.

Mami shook her head. "No, the Solarium will be out of bounds for renovation. Sorry."

Winnie was about to complain, but Ingrid spoke up first.

"It's okay, Mamita," she said, hugging Mami. "We'll keep ourselves entertained somewhere else."

Ingrid always seemed to know how to make Mami smile.

"Thank you for being so understanding," Paloma said.

"I'm starting to get a headache. Maybe plan a joke or two to tell me later?"

"Or maybe we can bring a couple of goats to the house to make us laugh. What do you think?" Ingrid asked.

"Goats?" Mami's face lit with amusement. "Now, how didn't I think of that? What do you say, Alice?"

Mami and the chief of staff laughed.

Winnie tried to think of something funny to add, but she gave up when all she could think of were sarcastic-sounding comments. How did Ingrid do it?

Not wanting to be less helpful in any way, Winnie took her mom's other hand and said, "Maybe not goats, but we promise we'll bring you some *fun*, Mamita. Right, Ingrid?"

"At least make it fun for Zora and Skylar. You don't remember how hard it can be to move into this house, but I certainly do. Give them a nice welcome, okay?"

Ingrid held Winnie's meaningful gaze for three or four seconds and then said, "Oh, Mami, we'll give them a welcome they'll never forget."

SKYLAR

THE NEXT DAY

The world as she knew it was ending, and honestly, Skylar wasn't ready. Not yet.

Ever since she could remember, Mom had been strict about keeping up with the planned schedule. Life with twins and a super-intense double-full-time job demanded it. But now that she was the President-Elect of the United States, the first Black woman ever to be chosen as president, things had reached a new level of stress and high-stakes decisions.

After that fateful day in November, a steep learning curve had followed. But a few weeks in, Skylar and her sister, Zora, had fallen into a routine of sorts. School, piano lessons, interviews, packing the house in Baltimore where they'd been so happy for ten years, planning outfits, learning etiquette, researching schools, etc., etc. Every second of the Williamses family time was accounted for. Why the change of plans?

"We're moving to the White House *tomorrow*? Why?" Skylar asked, trying to sound excited. Because she was excited about it. She really was. She'd been so looking forward to it after Winnie López had told her about the bowling alley, the fantastic pool, the chocolate cake on demand, and all the other amazing perks of living in the executive mansion.

"It's a lot for Mom to travel back and forth from DC, every weekend. Don't you miss her?" Zora said.

"Yes, I miss seeing her. Still . . ."

Zora shrugged and continued packing her duffel bag.

Skylar turned around and walked into her room.

She had mentally prepared herself for the big move well after the New Year, not tomorrow. Now all her preparation was crumbling into smithereens.

Tears and a tantrum might have helped her if she'd been four years old. But at twelve, she had to make do with a princess-style flouncy flop on her bed for some soul-cleansing crying.

If only she could text Winnie and Ingrid to ask for last-minute pointers! But her phone and Zora's had been taken away weeks ago. Something to do with national security.

Later, when her mom peeked into her room, Skylar made an effort to look as cool as Zora. After all, Mom had a million things to do, but she hadn't sent an assistant to check on her.

Skylar smiled, but the tears dropped of their own accord.

"Why so sad, Sky?"

Mom knew her so well, but in this case, she was a little off the mark.

"I'm not sad." Skylar took a shuddering breath and dabbed at her eyes daintily so she wouldn't smear the waterproof mascara she wasn't really allowed to wear yet. "But I'm not ready. What if we leave something important behind, Mom? What if the López girls don't really like me? I'm not finished reading the etiquette manual Alice Sung suggested. . . ."

Mom smiled. "What do you mean they won't like you? Everyone loves you. Just be yourself. And Sky, I hope that instead of worrying about what people think of you, you remember to cherish those around you. Don't stress over how to shine brighter than others. Wonder how you can help people find their own light."

Now, sitting in the back of the black limo that was driving her family toward the adventure of their lives, Skylar felt her light dimming.

She cherished her family, and more than anything, she wanted to live up to people's expectations so she wouldn't let her family down. The López girls made it look so easy, never straying off the perfect first-daughter script.

If there was such a thing, Alice Sung hadn't forwarded it with the other paperwork.

Skylar sat on top of her hands, the leather seats cool and soft on her skin, calming her down. From her window, the District of Columbia was a blur of naked trees and gray buildings. The motorcade zipped by, blocking intersections.

Her cheeks burned when she imagined what the people waiting in their cars were thinking of her and her family as they sat waiting for the motorcade to drive by. Were they upset her mom, a Black woman, had won and not the other candidate? Would her dad be okay in his role as the first-ever first gentleman? Would the media report on every single thing Skylar and her sister ever did, the way they did with Ingrid and Winnie?

The whole team around Mom had been very good at keeping the girls out of the spotlight for as long as possible, but their pictures—and not very flattering pictures, either—had ended up on every magazine cover. Skylar hated that the press was fixated on deciding who the twins looked like, their mother or their father. They were a perfect combination of both! They had Mom's tight curly hair, Dad's hazel eyes, and a mixture of features that was all their own.

But what bothered her the most was how the press called them *the twins*. As if learning their names was too hard, as if they were the only twins to ever live in the White House. Okay, there had only been one pair before, Jenna and Barbara Bush, but still, they weren't identical.

"Are you okay, Sky?" Mom asked, sending Skylar a worried look from the seat across from hers.

Insides still twisting, Skylar replied, "I'm okay."

"Look at it as a soft inauguration," Dad said, gently pressing her hand. Their skin was the same shade of dark brown, but she, Zora, and Dad were very different from each other!

Skylar tried to let his words comfort her. After all, he knew about this kind of thing. He'd taken an extended break from his acting when Mom's political career took off, and he'd been at plenty of red carpets and special events. Now his dark brown hair was shorter than usual, but like always, his eyes sparkled with pride every time he looked at Mom. Being in the spotlight was easy for him, but he didn't have any trouble yielding it to Mom or smiling and serving up looks for the cameras. Skylar wished his confidence was transferable.

This was such a history-making day, and Skylar hoped she wouldn't do anything to embarrass her family.

"You girls did a great job choosing your outfits," Dad said. "I'm glad you reached a compromise that made both of you—and Charlotte—happy."

Zora rolled her eyes, but Skylar brushed a hand over the luxurious camel's hair woolen coat she'd chosen after hours and hours of studying catalogs and websites. Charlotte was Skylar's favorite stylist. She'd never made a negative comment about not knowing how to do their hair, like some others. Under her direction, the girls chose dresses that fit their personalities. Skylar's was a simple yet elegant silky cream shift and Zora's was a gauzy navy with subtle purple hues.

"At least we didn't have to match," Zora said, loosening the collar of her black coat.

Skylar agreed. "We're way past that age," she said with an exaggerated shudder.

"But I miss those days!" Mom said with a wistful smile.

"Our shoes match," Skylar said, pointing her foot forward. She would have preferred a slight heel, but Zora had literally put her foot down and insisted on sensible, boring black ballerina flats.

A mechanical voice on a walkie-talkie broke their conversation.

"White House ahead. Everyone in position."

Zora tugged at the little book necklace charm Skylar had made for her last year.

"Is it too tight, Zora?" Skylar asked.

Her sister shook her head. "No, it's perfect. Thank you."

Skylar tried to smile, but her stomach clenched. She felt like she was falling into a technicolor whirlpool that pulled her deeper and deeper the more she tried to stay afloat. There was no other choice than to let go, let the current take her, let destiny unfold.

She took a deep breath and smiled tentatively, and slowly, she lit up from the outside in. This trick Dad had taught her always worked.

Not for nothing had the Secret Service given her the code name Twinkle.

Zora exclaimed, "I can see it! The White House is really . . . white!"

Mom and Dad shared an amused look, and then Mom's eyes turned back to their new home, which loomed through the foggy December cold. What was she thinking? What was she feeling?

There was no time to ask.

Skylar looked at her precious family: her dad, her mom, her sister—and a swell of emotion rose in her chest. This was the moment.

The car stopped. Agent Clarissa Lee, a tall Secret Service woman in a dark suit and earpiece, opened the door and nodded at Mom.

Skylar and Zora squirmed in their seats.

"Patience, girls," Skylar's dad reminded them playfully. "Mom goes first."

"I know, Daddy," Skylar said, flashing him one of her charming smiles. "The best for last, though, right?"

Mom checked herself on a tiny mirror and retouched her makeup. She swiped a dark curl out of her eyes. She took a deep breath, and her boss-lady expression fell into place before she stepped out of the car.

Dad winked at the girls and followed Mom.

For a second, it was just Zora and Skylar alone in the car. Together as always, since the beginning, inseparable. Usually nothing fazed Zora. But now she had a deer-in-the-headlights look, and Skylar knew she had to step up to lift her sister in her moment of need.

"Let's get them, tigress," Skylar urged Zora, who looked more like a skittish kitten at the moment.

Zora smiled nervously and got out of the car. Skylar followed her family.

The four of them stood side by side in front of the White House, the parents in the middle, and the girls at each end. Cameras clicked like an army of crickets. When a burst of polar wind made her eyes water, Skylar blinked softly so she wouldn't shed a tear by accident and give the world the wrong impression.

Using another one of Dad's tricks, she tried to divert the warmth from her chest to the rest of her body. Skylar threw her hair back, put the shine on her smile, and did her princess wave at the crowd, trying to ignore the gallop of her heart.

As they had practiced, Mom held Zora's hand, and Daddy held Skylar's.

Together, they took that first step into the land of no return.

ZORA

As a budding historian, Zora knew the footage of their arrival in the White House would be replayed into infinity, dissected and distorted for a glimpse into the Williams family.

Although she had a photographic memory, later she wouldn't remember the walk from the black car to the White House entrance where the entire López family was waiting.

Everything seemed like a dream in which she only recognized flashes and bursts of color.

The flag waving in the frigid wind. The swarm of serious, black-uniformed Secret Service agents frantically speaking into their headsets. The green wreaths decorating the stair banister that she could see from the front door of the White House. The navy blue of her mom's suit as she resolutely walked toward her destiny as the first woman to be president-elect of the United States of America. And a Black woman at that.

But the most vivid image in Zora's mind was her sister's dazzling smile as she waved at the reporters like a Disney princess. Zora slowed down her steps to watch her. They might look the same, but their souls couldn't be more different.

"Smile, Skylar!" a reporter called, looking at Zora, who couldn't stop herself from frowning.

But her sister continued walking without breaking her stride, and she replied with a dimpled smile, *"I'm* Skylar!"

Everyone said there was no such thing as a perfect family, but in most people's eyes, the First Family meant a Perfect Family. Standing in front of the president, the first lady, and their two daughters in their flawless glory, Zora realized that Winnie and Ingrid had set a high bar for beauty, grace, smarts, and charm.

Skylar wouldn't have any problems charming anyone.

But if the press kept confusing them and Zora didn't pull her weight, then her sister's efforts would be for nothing, which wasn't fair in the least.

Zora made herself smile, but her face was stiff with cold and nerves.

"Welcome home, President-Elect Williams and family," President López said.

The grown-ups shook hands, and the four girls looked at each other, hesitating.

Zora couldn't remember if they should shake hands or if it was okay to hug. They hadn't seen each other for a while, but they were friends, after all. So she took the first step and hugged the López sister closest to her. Ingrid.

"Hi! It's so great to see you!" And then Zora added with a whisper, "I'm Zora." She felt like she had to clarify, in case Ingrid was confused.

"I know," Ingrid said. "I recognized you from the book charm."

Zora tugged at her charm again and then turned to hug Winnie, who looked as uncomfortable in the spotlight as Zora felt.

Around her, the cameras kept clicking.

"Please come in," Mrs. López said.

Stepping through the hallowed entrance of the most famous residence in the world, Zora felt as if she was walking into a sacred building, like a church or a library.

The White House was a living museum. But from now on, it was also her home.

At home, they'd always taken their shoes off.

"Shoes off?" she asked softly.

Ingrid laughed as if Zora had told a joke and continued walking ahead of the group.

"I guess that's a no," Skylar whispered as she followed the others.

Zora filed all this information carefully. There was so much to learn, and she was excited to learn it. It was just that there were so many little details.

If only there was a way that the house could transfer its secrets instantaneously. If only she could place her hand on the walls for them to tell her all she needed to know to be loved and live up to everyone's expectations!

The ballerina flats were pinching her big toes, and she tried not to limp or wince. She couldn't blame anyone but herself for choosing the most uncomfortable shoes ever. She couldn't wait to take them off. At the appropriate time, of course. She followed her family across the Reception Room and craned her neck to get a peek at the layout of the house she'd studied online. Things looked different live than on video, but she saw the shelves lining the walls of a room on the right.

"Look!" she said, pointing. "The Library!"

Ingrid hooked her arm in Zora's and in a tourist-guide voice said, "Yes, the White House's Library was created by First Lady Abigail Fillmore. I'll show you later."

Zora's heart leaped with excitement. She wouldn't be getting her own books until the official move-in day in

January, but she couldn't wait to go explore the library, losing herself in books, the best friends a girl could ever have.

"I just can't wait to see our rooms!" Skylar said.

Winnie narrowed her eyes and said, "You know what? That's an excellent idea! Let's get away from this."

Zora and Skylar looked at their parents, who were again posing with the Lópezes.

"We're leaving. Is that okay?" Winnie asked.

Mrs. López nodded, still smiling for the photographers. "Of course. Let's meet up for dinner. Be on time."

Zora's mom, who already looked like she'd always belonged in these rooms, said, "We have a few meetings. You two have fun."

"Have fun," Dad echoed before following the president, the first lady, and their mom to a tea room with the most magnificent Christmas tree Zora had seen in her life.

"And behave!" President López called out.

Zora turned around just in time to see him smile and wink at her. She'd always liked him. She smiled back.

"Finally on our own! I can't wait to show you everything!" Ingrid exclaimed, pulling Zora away from the Secret Service agents posted along the hall and at the tea room's entrance.

"On our own?" Skylar asked, sending Zora an amused look.

All around them, ushers and maids were going about

their jobs. A reporter with a camera followed the girls' every move. The hallway alone teemed with people.

Zora swallowed the knot growing in her throat. The sensory overload was intense.

Ingrid was saying something about a tour, but to Zora, the words blurred until it all sounded like the buzzing of bees.

Winnie seemed to sense what was happening, because she said, "Easy, Ingrid. Let Zora breathe for a sec. This"—she motioned with her head toward the Secret Service agents stationed like soldiers next to the door and at each end of the hallways—"can be too much. You don't remember what it's like to walk in here for the first time, but I do."

"But this is the best thing that's ever happened to us," Skylar said, looking around her with sparkling eyes.

Winnie shrugged. "Even the best things can be overwhelming. Trust me."

The older López girl was always so composed and proper. Zora wanted to ask her about how she dealt with so many demands from so many directions. But her questions would have to wait.

Ingrid was tapping her foot and snapping her fingers. "Let's go on a tour!" She had a clipboard under her arm. Zora hadn't seen her grab it.

"Yes, let's head upstairs," Winnie said.

Ingrid cleared her throat and said, "Just so you know, there are eight staircases—"

"And three elevators," Zora added. She'd read about it online.

Ingrid's shoulders fell like she was deflating with disappointment that Zora already knew this.

"Sorry," Zora said, and Ingrid gave a little shrug.

Skylar was looking at her outfit in a giant gilded mirror and had missed the whole thing.

"Let's go," Winnie said.

Ingrid followed her sister.

The reporter stayed downstairs as if he was unable to cross an invisible line.

In an uncomfortable silence, Zora trailed behind Winnie, Ingrid, and Skylar, making an effort not to gasp in awe at the portraits of the house's residents, modern and historic, and the elegant but homey holiday decorations.

"Welcome home!" Ingrid said when they reached the landing.

The scent of orange and sage made this floor way cozier than the downstairs. Zora was surprised to see a quaint sitting corner with comfy-looking chairs. She hadn't really known what to expect in the residence.

Zora's feet throbbed, and she asked, "Can we take our shoes off now?"

"Of course! Let me take your coats!" Ingrid helped Skylar out of her coat and scarf, and taking Zora's too, she draped them on one of the chairs.

"We brought a change of clothes," Zora said. The dress was making her neck itch. She longed for a soft T-shirt and jeans, like the López girls were wearing. "But we left the bags in the car."

"Do you want to borrow something?" Winnie asked.

Before Zora could say anything, Skylar shook her head. "No, thanks! Being here is like being in a fairy tale!" Her eyes shone. "I feel like a princess all dressed up."

Zora, who knew how some real fairy tales ended, shivered. Especially when she noticed the López girls exchanging another cryptic look. She hoped they weren't offended Skylar had rejected their offer for comfy clothes. Zora would have happily accepted, but she didn't know how to do that now without betraying her sister.

"It's great to see the residence section of the house," she said, and her voice sounded a little like she was choking. "It's pretty much impossible to find specific details online."

"Were you stalking our house, Zora?" Ingrid asked, and laughed, apparently at Zora's embarrassment. "Let's go. I'll show you your rooms."

"It wasn't stalking. It was research—"

Skylar sent her a pointed look, and Zora wanted to fold in on herself.

Once again, Zora trailed behind the other girls along a long corridor lined with miniature Christmas trees.

Suddenly a pungent smell replaced the elegant scent from the landing.

"What's that . . . stink?" Zora asked, waving a hand in front of her nose.

Winnie's face was like a mask, and Ingrid raised her eyebrows and said, "That would be First Ferret Lafayette. He sleeps in Winnie's room, and yep . . . his cage is in need of a major clean-up."

Winnie blushed to the tips of her ears. "I've been busy, okay?" She stood at the mouth of a hallway, which the floor plans Zora had studied called the Closet Hall. It had a door at the end and one on either side, which looked like they led to the girls' bedrooms. "We had such short notice about you girls moving in."

"Do you want us to help you clean it?" Zora asked.

Her sister sent her an alarmed look and shuffled back, as if she wanted to put as much distance from the ferret as possible. Once again Zora regretted speaking without thinking things through. She usually didn't have this problem. Maybe Ingrid's chattiness was catching.

"Thanks, but no thanks," Winnie said. "He's not used to other people, and he can't really run around the house. Especially not now, with a lot of strangers around."

The uncomfortable silence fell on the girls again, and

this time, Skylar spoke first. "Sorry . . . we didn't mean to . . . I'm sure this is hard for you, too. We only found out we were moving yesterday."

Winnie's face turned flaming red, and she looked at her sister as if asking for help.

"It's not your fault this happened so suddenly. It can't be easy for you either," Ingrid said. "Anyway, these are *our* rooms." She pointed ahead but didn't invite them in. "We'll show them to you later, once Win does her chores. The presidential suite is at the end of the Closet Hall, but no visitors are allowed there. Follow me now."

They continued walking along the central corridor. Skylar looked like Christmas had been canceled. She'd been waiting to see the rooms forever. Knowing her sister, Zora was convinced that Sky was already planning how to change things around to make the place theirs. She'd been so close, and then Zora had had to comment about the ferret's smell and offend their hosts.

"And this is where we plot to rule the world," Ingrid said when they arrived at a comfortable living room with blankets, beanbags, and pillows of bright designs and colors.

Skylar was about to sit on one of the beanbags, when Ingrid ran to her and, snatching the blanket on top of it, said, "Sorry. This is my favorite blanket. I don't know why it's here."

Winnie rolled her eyes. "At least you can let her borrow

it, Ingrid. It's not like—"

She stopped talking when a petite lady dressed in elegant black slacks, white shirt, and a black bow tie approached the group. She had beautiful auburn hair pulled back and a smattering of freckles on her smiling face.

"How about some hot chocolate, girls? It's freezing out there!"

Before they could reply, another woman was placing a tray with a pitcher of steaming hot chocolate, four mugs, and a plate of small sandwiches on the table.

"Thank you!" Skylar said, beaming. "Look, Zora! Our names on the mugs!"

Zora was impressed. She'd never owned a mug with her own name, which, after all, wasn't exactly common.

"Thank you," Zora echoed, marveling at the card on the tray. It read *Zora and Skylar, Welcome to the White House!* in cheerful sparkly letters.

"You did this?" Skylar asked, gazing at the card with shiny eyes.

Zora's chest warmed at the lovely detail. And here she'd been thinking that she was an inconvenience in the López girls' lives, that the chemistry they'd had during the campaign had been lost. How wrong had she been!

"We didn't exactly make them, but we planned it," Ingrid replied, smiling. "Leo in Calligraphy helped us bring it to life."

"Everyone is so happy to have you, girls," the petite woman said.

"We are!" Winnie said, but her voice sounded too high-pitched to be genuine. "And thanks for preparing this, Kate. You're the best." She turned to Zora and Skylar and said, "This is Kate. She's one of our favorites here, and always brings the best treats."

Ingrid hugged Kate and said, "We're going to miss you, Kate!"

Zora hadn't known if she could hug the house staff, but being a hugger, she felt comforted knowing that the people working in the house felt like family to the López girls.

Kate smiled brightly and patted Ingrid's head. "You don't even know how much I'm going to miss *you*, missy!" And then she turned to Zora and Skylar, who looked unsure of what to do. "And it will be my pleasure to spoil you girls too! I can't wait until we learn what you like, your favorite treats and meals and such. The whole staff hopes your stay as guests is just the start of wonderful years as residents ahead. We're all very much looking forward to getting to know you."

She left, and there was a charged silence.

"Now please sit down and eat!" Ingrid urged. She was smiling, but her eyes were shiny, and Zora had a hunch Ingrid had been on the verge of crying, for some reason. "Then we'll see the rest of the house!"

Zora sat at the table without saying a word. She didn't understand why their interactions had felt so tense ever since they'd walked into the house.

The girls ate in silence, and Zora's mind scrambled for some trivia to break the ice.

Apparently she wasn't the only one who'd been trying to start a conversation.

"I hope it doesn't stay cloudy for too long," Ingrid said, as if the quiet physically hurt her.

"I know," said Skylar. "I can't wait for spring to be here and to see the gardens. When they look pretty, that is."

Ingrid's jaw clenched. "They look beautiful now too. Just different."

Zora nibbled at her sandwich and took small sips of her drink. The hot chocolate was delicious but a tad too sweet. Not like she'd say anything.

Finally, when Zora had started to relax, Winnie said, "If everyone's finished, we can get going."

Zora tried to gather her cup and plate to put them away, but Kate reappeared and said, "What great manners! But leave that to us, love. We'll take care of it."

Zora realized there were two other attendants waiting just out of sight to pick up after her and the other girls. She hesitated a second but then realized that this was these people's job, and she'd better get used to being waited on. It was a weird experience to think this was their way of life now. They'd always had help at home from a cleaning and laundry service, but never like this.

While she processed how her life would go on for the next four years, the girls were gone.

Once again Zora was chasing after them, this time to the third floor.

Winnie and Skylar were quietly talking about the rooms. Zora strained to hear better.

"Yours are right off the Solarium, and your parents will be across from you on the Center Hall," Winnie said. "Mami said this way you'd have more privacy. But in the meantime, you can choose which rooms will be yours after we move out in January."

With the clipboard again under an arm, Ingrid showed them the gym, the Music Room, and the Greenhouse, then snuck them into the Solarium. Although the sky was still a leaden gray, seen from the floor-to-ceiling windows, Washington covered in snow looked like a postcard. With a jolt, Zora remembered that Jackie Kennedy had set up a kindergarten for her children in this place.

"The light is lovely," Ingrid said. "But in the middle of summer, it feels like a sauna."

As Ingrid explained to her how to work the window shades, Zora could only smile and nod.

"Now, follow me," Ingrid said. "I want to show you your rooms. They're right on this hallway."

"Finally!" Skylar exclaimed, following Winnie.

But the older López girl turned and said, "Sorry. Ingrid will guide you. I need to do something. I'll meet you in a minute." She left before anyone could ask anything else.

Ingrid showed them to their rooms, which were sensibly decorated, like those at a chic hotel, only cozier.

"I thought my sister and I were sharing," Zora said.

Ingrid looked alarmed. "Oh! Did you want to share? I can tell my mom you prefer—"

"No, no. It's okay this way. I need my alone time," she said, laughing and waving a hand.

Skylar sent her a thumbs-up. "At least we're close together."

Suddenly Zora felt so tired, she wished she could have a few minutes to recover on her own. Did Winnie too feel like she needed alone time? Was that why she'd left?

She yawned, hoping Ingrid would get the hint. But the López girl was tapping her foot again, waiting to resume the tour.

Zora didn't have the heart to stay in her room. Besides, Skylar was already following Ingrid back to the first floor.

Winnie joined them, but she didn't explain what she'd been doing.

"Usually we don't even dream of going to the first floor at this time of day, but there are no visitors today. During the holidays, thousands of people will go through the house. Sometimes Win and I have to wait until the nighttime to look at the decorations. Come, you need to see the gingerbread-house village Jean-Paul made this year!"

Zora had no idea who Jean-Paul was, but when she saw his re-creation of the iconic Washington, DC, buildings, made out of gingerbread and icing, she said, "Jean-Paul must be a magician!"

The little details on the gingerbread White House were so intricate, she marveled at his skill.

"Did he include the secret tunnels underneath the house in this replica?" Zora asked.

Ingrid laughed. "Not only have you been stalking the house, Zora, but you've also been duped by conspiracy theories."

She shrugged. "Even conspiracies can start from a kernel of truth. . . . Just sayin'."

Ingrid rolled her eyes, not even hiding her annoyance anymore. "For the record, there's no such thing as secret tunnels. Winnie and I would know all about them, right, Win?"

But when Zora looked behind her, face burning, she realized that Winnie and her sister had moved on to the East Room, where everything glittered and sparkled. Skylar twirled in the center of the room, her arms spread out.

The most perfect flower arrangement Zora had ever seen sat on a table, and she couldn't resist its pull. The roses and lilies didn't look real, and Zora brushed a finger over them to see if they were artificial or not. The petals were plump and soft. Definitely real. Like the rest of the house, the East Room was decorated with wreaths and garlands. A beautiful grand piano was angled against the wall where the famous Washington portrait was displayed.

"Oh, the portrait!" Zora exclaimed, and when she realized how loud she'd been, she pressed her hands to her mouth.

"She's been studying about it," Skylar explained, shaking her head.

"Ay, Zora, you didn't even give me the chance to introduce it to you!" Ingrid said, and before Zora could apologize once again for ruining the surprise, Ingrid added in a high-pitched voice, and in the same exact intonation Zora had heard tour guides use, "Behold, George Washington!"

"It looks way bigger in person than on a screen. "She hadn't planned on saying anything negative about the Founding Fathers, but she couldn't help herself.

"Washington would not be thrilled to see my sister and me living in this house. . . . You know what I mean?"

Winnie nodded with a knowing smile. "Nope."

She seemed to know her history, then, and Zora liked her the more for it.

Ingrid took out a disposable camera from her pocket

and said, "For that reason, let me take a picture of you! Mami took our phones so we couldn't post anything non-approved on social media about today."

Zora understood the feeling. "We can't get our phones back until they get specially refurbished or something."

Ingrid's face brightened. "Mami gave us these cameras, though. So we could remember this moment forever. You know, pics or it didn't happen."

Although she didn't feel like it, Zora posed for the pictures, following Ingrid's instructions to imitate Washington's gesture with his open hand and making a motion like she was showing off a table laden for a party.

"You know this is a replica, right?" Zora said, unable to hold on any longer without showing off what she'd learned about the White House. "Dolley Madison saved the original from a fire that broke out during the War of 1812."

"Oh . . . Dolley! Yes, I heard about her." Ingrid's cheeks were bright red, like she didn't actually know who Dolley Madison was. "She saved it, then? Wow."

"Actually, Paul Jennings did. Her 'personal servant,'" she said, using air quotes, like Ingrid had done before. "He wrote the first White House memoir, did you know?"

Ingrid looked impressed. "Get out of here! I must have passed this painting like a million times in the eight years I've lived here!" Ingrid exclaimed. "I mean, I've eaves-dropped on more tours than I could count, but I never heard this tidbit. Is that another one of your conspiracy theories?"

"First of all, they're not *my* conspiracy theories. And second of all, that's regular history, and some of things we learn in school are wrong or incomplete. I read a lot," Zora said. She felt herself blush to the tips of her ears. All the trivia she'd accumulated bubbled inside her, and with her excitement to be here, it was hard to contain. She didn't have the speech rate Ingrid possessed, but she had endurance, and honestly, she could talk about history for hours and hours. "So many extraordinary people have lived in this house."

"So many!" Ingrid said, looking at the portraits lining the walls. "And now your mom is the first woman to become the president of the United States. An epic jefa, my dad says! She's forever a part of history now, which means you and your sister are . . . *historic!*"

Zora detected a hint of something hostile in Ingrid's voice, but she couldn't put her finger on it. Jealousy? But that was ridiculous! Why would Ingrid be jealous of Zora?

She was about to ask Skylar to go to the bathroom with her, so she could ask for her sister's opinion, when a big clock chimed somewhere in the house.

In that moment, one of the ushers approached them and announced, "It's time for dinner, ladies."

Ingrid wasn't hungry after the extra-sweet hot chocolate, but this was one of those moments that required duty before want or even need.

"Do you think it's okay if we wear the same dresses?" Skylar asked. "I wonder when our duffels will be sent up. Can we go check?"

But one of the Secret Service men was calling them over, tapping at his watch.

"Let's go, Zora," Skylar said, draping an arm over her sister's shoulders.

They were heading to the second floor when one of the attendants called out, "This way, girls!" She pointed to a formal dining room.

"But my shoes are upstairs," Zora said, just noticing she'd been barefoot the whole time.

"I'll go get them!" Winnie said, and took off before Zora could decide to come along.

A few minutes later, Winnie slid off the staircase railing and gracefully landed in front of Zora with the shoes in her hand.

"Here they are," she said.

"Thank you, Win. You saved me."

"Of course," Winnie said.

Zora put on her shoes and immediately regretted having taken them off. They pinched her more than ever.

Together, they headed to the State Dining Room.

Zora had read all about all the renovations to this room, how it had changed through the years. But like everything at the White House, it was one thing to read about something and quite another to be in it. Almost like jumping inside a book or a movie. She followed Ingrid and Winnie.

As soon as the girls stepped into the dining room, reserved for the most exclusive meetings, Zora caught another look passing between Ingrid and Winnie. The López girls seemed to be having a silent argument, but Zora didn't have a chance to find out what it was all about.

The Lópezes and the Williamses weren't the only people in the room. By now, Zora should've been used to sharing her parents with other people and not having private meals that often, but a part of her had hoped that, at least for the first night, there would be a small dinner, something resembling normal.

Instead, she counted at least ten other adult couples and a few people who looked like the couples' children, although no one was as young as twelve. When they walked in, everyone turned in her and Skylar's direction.

Winnie muttered, "It will be okay, trust me."

Zora tried to turn off her introvert self and channel all her best manners, smiling, answering questions, trying to give the best first impression.

All the while, the ever-present clicking of cameras and requests to "Smile!" had her whipping her face this way and that until her cheeks hurt from smiling so much and her mouth went dry from talking nonstop.

She was good at reciting trivia, but all in moderation, and today had been eleventy million hours long already. She was ready for some well-deserved quiet time.

But first they had to survive their first dinner at the White House.

All the young people had been assigned to seats at the end of the table, the only two boys present each placed between a Williams and a López sister.

Zora sat next to a boy of about fourteen who looked familiar, like someone from TV is familiar. And handsome. Ingrid was on his other side. Skylar and Winnie were across the table, and Zora tried to catch her sister's eye to see if she recognized the cute boy. But Skylar was busy talking to Winnie and the boy sitting between them. He was cute in his own way, dark haired and freckly. He had a pin with the Canadian flag on the lapel of his jacket, and finally she remembered him. Edmund, the Canadian prime minister's nephew. But before she could ask him what it was like to live at 24 Sussex, where the government residence was located in the neighboring country, Ingrid reached over and tapped her shoulder to get her attention.

Zora jumped.

"Hola, Javi," Ingrid said, doing a fun handshake with the handsome boy. "Let me introduce you to Zora, one of President-Elect Williams's daughters. Zora, this is Javi Rojas."

At the mention of his full name, Zora immediately realized who the boy was. "Your dad is a reporter. Carlos!" she exclaimed. "We met him during the campaign. Is he here?"

Javi had a charming smile, and Zora blushed in spite of herself. "I'm certainly Carlos's son, and yes, he's here. He's sitting farther up the table, talking to the presidents. I guess this is the unofficial kiddie section."

"I noticed that too," Zora said.

"How've you been, Javi?" Ingrid asked. "You haven't been around in forever." She patted his face and narrowed her eyes. "Let me guess. You've been sunning in beautiful San Juan?"

Javi laughed. He had perfect white teeth and sharp dark brown eyes. "I was just there last week, visiting my mom for Thanksgiving. Now I'm busy with school. But guess what!"

"What?" Ingrid and Zora asked in unison.

He shrugged one shoulder, adorably. "I got my first assignment from *Verified Teen* magazine."

Zora was impressed. *Verified Teen* was her favorite.

Ingrid nodded like a proud little sister. "Look at you, Javi! What is it about?"

He shrugged again. He glanced across the table at Winnie and Skylar, and said, "The four of you, actually. The first daughters at the White House."

Blood rushed to Zora's head.

But before Ingrid or Javi could add anything, President López clinked on a cup to call everyone's attention.

The room went quiet.

"President-Elect Theresa Williams, First Gentleman Beau Williams, and Zora and Skylar, welcome to our home, which we will be sharing for the next several weeks. May this be the first day of an unforgettable time in your lives and the destiny of our nation. Salud!" He lifted his champagne flute, and everyone else joined him in the toast.

Zora took a sip of the fancy orange drink in front of her. It tasted like mandarin soda. The ice cube clinked against her teeth. But before she put the glass down, Skylar's high-pitched scream startled her.

In that moment, Zora saw a pair of tiny eyes inside her glass. In a reflex movement, she flung the rest of the drink right at Javi.

He gasped as the orange drink seeped through the immaculate white shirt he was wearing. Javi bolted out of the room before Zora could apologize.

On the other side of the table, Skylar was babbling. "There's a bug in my glass."

As soon as people understood what she was saying, three attendants rushed to the table to check on the glasses.

From the corner of her eye, Zora saw an English lord surreptitiously check on his two glasses, the one with water and the other with wine. He must have been satisfied, because he took a sip of water and blotted his forehead with a cream-colored handkerchief. Still, he sent the girls a disapproving look.

Zora's eyes flew to her mom, who was a waxy shade of gray next to Dad. He didn't say anything, but in his eyes, Zora read his question. *Are you okay?*

"It's only an ice cube with Laffy's face on it, miss," one of the attendants said. He was a nice Latino man with soft velvety eyes. He showed her the ice cube he held on the palm of his hand.

Ingrid grabbed it to show Zora better. "It's a little image of Laffy saying welcome. It's printed on sugary paper. It's safe to eat. There's one in my drink too, see?"

Across the table, Skylar was laughing to cover for screaming, because the photographers wouldn't stop taking pictures. Zora didn't even want to imagine what the tabloids and social media would say about this dinner tomorrow.

"Whose idea was this? Why?" Zora asked.

"It was a cute joke," Winnie said, her eyes darting to the end of the table where her parents sat. "A harmless welcome joke, in the best White House tradition."

Winnie's words sounded totally natural and sincere, but Zora felt betrayed, and embarrassed about her reaction.

She had read about the infamous pranks the outgoing

administration had sometimes played on the incoming one, but she'd never expected this.

Ingrid was covering her face with a napkin. Then she dropped it and, looking truly repentant, said, "I'm sorry, Zora. It was just a joke. Everyone in this section of the table had the same ice cubes. We didn't think you'd be scared. It was supposed to be cute."

Zora didn't want to cry in front of everyone. So instead of lashing out, she summoned a bright smile that was worthy of Skylar and said, "It's all good, Ingrid. Don't worry about it. All for tradition, right?"

Ingrid smiled shyly, and soon the conversation resumed. Most people seemed to forget all about the incident. Zora pretended to put it behind her, but later, when dinner was over and they were waiting for their parents so they could finally go to their rooms, she asked her sister, "Are you okay?"

Skylar's cheeks went red. "I'm furious with myself. I'm sorry that I startled you and you threw your drink at that boy."

At the memory of the stain spreading on Javi's shirt, and the way he'd left the room, Zora felt like a tornado was roaring in her ears.

"I'm so embarrassed," she said, wishing she could turn back time.

"It wasn't your fault," Skylar whispered, and patted Zora's shoulder.

At the other end of the room, Ingrid and Winnie laughed with Edmund. Were they laughing at Zora and her sister?

She clenched her teeth. "No. It was *their* fault. Don't worry, Skylar. Those girls won't know what's coming to them. We're striking back."

INGRID

"Do you want to stay up and watch a movie?" Ingrid asked Zora. "We can have a late night."

Zora gave her a little smile and shook her head. "It's super late, and besides, we have to get ready for school tomorrow," she said before heading back next to her parents and sister.

Ingrid fidgeted in place, standing by herself. A few of the guests remained in the Visitors' Foyer, but not Javi. He'd never returned to dinner, and Ingrid had really wanted to ask about his assignment for *Verified Teen*.

In spite of the Williams girls' perfect smiles and don't-you-worries, Ingrid couldn't shake the nagging feeling that something had been off since they'd arrived at the

White House. The awkwardness between the two sets of sisters had turned into glacial cold after the misunderstanding with the ice cubes. Ingrid tried to salvage the day by doing what she always did when she was nervous and overwhelmed: making people laugh.

Choosing from her repertoire, she did an impersonation of her dad, hands on her hips and sighing. "My daughters, my daughters. I'm the president and they still don't obey me."

Her dad shook his head and bit his lip.

"What, is it time for the Ingrid Show?" he finally asked, but in his voice there was an edge of warning that Ingrid was about to cross a line.

She must have made a face, because Mr. Williams laughed, coming to her rescue. "You're too funny, Ingrid. I don't know where you kids get all that energy."

"From us," Ingrid's mom said, standing next to her.

Ingrid knew this was a sign for her to try to rein in her behavior, but still, her heart about burst with joy. Mr. Williams thought she was funny.

"I want to be a comedian when I grow up," she said, not knowing if it would be impolite to excuse herself and run to her room, or if she should continue the conversation. "Zora told me that at the beginning of your career you did stand-up. Is that right?"

When Mami quietly left to greet another guest, Ingrid

knew she'd asked the right question and felt a little better.

Mr. Williams was kind and gracious, and he answered all her questions, but Ingrid could feel the annoyed looks Zora and Skylar sent her way. When she turned around to glance over her shoulder, she caught a glimpse of the hurt expression on Zora's face. Ingrid's heart withered like a squashed spider.

She hadn't meant to humiliate the other girls. She felt terrible.

"Like everything, good comedy requires practice," Mr. Williams said. "It also requires compassion and kindness *and* timing. Don't forget that. Read the room."

"Of course," she said, chastised, and turned to look for Skylar and Zora to ask for forgiveness.

They were gone.

"Thank you," Ingrid added, just in time before Mr. Williams joined President-Elect Williams and together they headed up to the residence.

For the first time in her life, Ingrid wished for a time machine. Not to speed time forward but to turn it back just a bit and warn Skylar and Zora that the ice cubes were meant to be a joke, not even a prank.

"Compassion and kindness and timing. Don't forget that. Read the room."

"What happened?" Winnie asked, hooking her arm in

Ingrid's. "You look worried."

"I'll tell you upstairs," she said as they too followed the procession. They passed Alice, who was talking to Carlos Rojas. So that meant Javi could still be around.

"Good night, Alice. Chau, Carlos," Winnie said.

"I hope Javi's all right," Ingrid said, and Carlos started laughing.

Usually Ingrid loved to make people laugh. But now she blushed.

"Good night, girls," he said, and Alice added, "Behave, please."

They headed to Winnie's room. After closing the door behind her, Ingrid sat on the bed.

"I never thought they'd get scared," Winnie said, and bit her lip.

"I feel bad for Javi," Ingrid said.

"What were you guys talking about before the ice cube fiasco?"

"He's writing a piece for *Verified Teen*," Ingrid said. "About us. The four first daughters."

"Are you serious?" Winnie said, clasping her hands. "And he was there for the prank?"

Ingrid giggled, but her eyes filled with tears at the memory. "I feel so bad."

"What's he writing about us?" Winnie asked. Her voice

sounded cool, but Ingrid knew her sister had a platonic crush on Javi.

"He didn't have the chance to say," Ingrid said. "I hope he doesn't write about the ice-cube fiasco. . . ." She sighed. "Mami and Papi explicitly asked us to welcome Zora and Skylar and make tonight unforgettable."

Winnie plopped on the bed. "Well, if nothing else, the night will be memorable."

"I'm afraid they're mad at us," Ingrid said, cringing. If she'd seen a pair of googly eyes in her glass, she'd have been scared too. But she'd also take it as it was intended. A cute joke. "I guess they're now officially admitted to the First Kids Club, though. The other administrations do this—"

"The other administrations never stayed behind to see the incoming family's reactions." Winnie sat back up, hugging her crossed legs.

"What if they retaliate?" asked Ingrid.

"Retaliate?" asked Winnie.

"Strike back."

"I know what retaliate means!" Winnie exclaimed. "I meant, what can they do to us? Nothing. Besides, no one will remember about this tomorrow. It doesn't even qualify as a prank. Trust me." She kissed Ingrid on the cheek. "Everyone else laughed about it. They're just overreacting."

Ingrid got up to head to her room. "I hope you're right.

If not, we're in deep trouble. Seven weeks of awkwardness . . . and if Javi writes about it . . ."

"I'll text him tomorrow when we get our phones back. Don't worry," Winnie said. "Good night, Parrot, I mean Parakeet."

Ingrid smiled. "Good night, Explosive, I mean Popcorn."

Winnie aimed a pillow at her and threw it. Ingrid closed her sister's door just in time. But the smile slid off her face when she thought of Zora's expression. She went to bed wondering if the Williams family had changed their minds and were moving to a hotel in the middle of the night.

What if they decided that they'd just wait for the López troublemakers to be gone before moving in? What if the whole staff quit, appalled at the bad look they'd given the whole household? Had that ever happened before?

What if her last act as a first daughter ruined all the years of good memories?

She was really worried, but in the end, she fell asleep before her parents stopped by to say good night. Still, all night long, nightmares replayed her worst fear: the twins' revenge.

In one of her dreams, Zora and Skylar had covered all the soap bars in every bathroom with clear nail polish, and in the shower after soccer practice, when she was particularly stinky, Ingrid rubbed and rubbed the soap but couldn't manage to produce any suds. She had to show up at a fancy dinner with Javi in all her stinky glory.

She woke up with a start just when the glowing numbers on her nightstand clock marked two in the morning. She went back to sleep. This time, she dreamed that she was running late for school, and when she tried to rush out of her room, she found she couldn't cross the hallways because Zora and Skylar had lined the floor with tiny cups they'd gathered from all over the house and placed like booby traps. A neon-green liquid bubbled like acid in the cups. If it spilled, the antique floors would be ruined.

"No!!!!" Ingrid screamed, and woke up. This time the clock marked seven a.m.

It took a while for her heart rate to go back to normal.

Imagining her horror-struck face, she laughed. There was no way the girls would sneak into her bathroom to sabotage her hand soap. She'd been so silly! But she was impressed that her mind had come up with all these outrageous ideas to prank someone! Where had the nightmares come from?

Before the dreams fizzled out and she forgot crucial details, she hurriedly scribbled in her Book of Risas. Maybe in the new house, she'd play these tricks on Winnie for pulling her into such a mess.

Gingerly, Ingrid opened the door of her room, and to

her relief there were no miniature cups on the floor, waiting like a booby trap. Instead there was something worse. Her mom, quietly leaving Winnie's room with a stern expression on her face.

It was best to meet her fate instead of running away like she wanted to.

Ingrid blurted out, "Mami, I'm sorry about yesterday! I promise we never imagined it would backfire like that."

Paloma López yelped, startled. Ingrid clapped her hands on her mouth in horror at how she'd scared her mom. But instead of telling her off, once she had recovered, Mami rolled her eyes in such an out-of-character way that Ingrid couldn't help but laugh.

"I saw that, Mami!" Ingrid said, hugging her.

Paloma kissed the top of Ingrid's head. "Your sister is determined to beat Tad Lincoln for First Hellion status. How did she pull you along?"

Ingrid's heart clenched for her sister. She couldn't let her take all the blame. "Actually . . . I was the one who came up with the idea of a cute joke."

"She confessed the ice-cube thing was her idea."

"It was both of us," Ingrid said. "She's trying to be all noble about it."

"How in the world did you get Laffy's picture inside the ice cubes for the kids' drinks?"

Ingrid looked over toward the closet at the end of the

hall, where she and Winnie kept their art supplies and things they didn't want cluttering their rooms—like left-over Halloween stuff. "We got them last year for Laffy's birthday. You and Papi were on tour in Europe. I thought they were cute even inside the ice cubes."

Paloma sighed resignedly. "They were cute, but put yourself in the girls' place. So many new things in one day . . ."

"Mami, we didn't mean to—"

"I know, Ingrid. But remember, we need simplicity and peace the last few days here. There are too many people, too many styles of doing things. Let's not complicate our lives during our last weeks at this house and end on a bad note. Besides, how many times do I have to tell you the significance of two Latina girls and two Black girls living in the White House? A lot of people aren't happy about that. They'll look for any excuse to make—"

"Racist comments?" Ingrid asked, shrugging.

Mami sighed, closing her eyes. "Yes, mi amor. Racist comments. Think about the repercussions!"

Ingrid's spirits fell, like they did every time she remembered she had only a handful of days left in this beloved place. "I'm sorry, Mami. I didn't mean to."

Mami tapped Ingrid's chin and said, "Actions have consequences, even if you had the best intentions. After you two apologize, I want no more funny business. Está claro?"

Of course it was clear, and just in case, Ingrid feigned an expression of solemnity that made her mom laugh.

"Go have breakfast and then get ready for school," Mami said, and headed to her office.

In the eat-in kitchen at the end of the West Sitting Hall, there was no trace of the Williams girls, and Ingrid was both low-key disappointed and a little relieved. For all she knew, they were having breakfast in the Solarium or with their parents, although judging by Papi's schedule, President-Elect Williams must already have been hard at work from the early hours of the morning.

With Zora and Skylar out of the picture, Ingrid could maybe figure out a way to properly apologize to the Williams sisters. But deep in her heart, she hoped they were preparing their revenge. How fun would that be? They'd need inside help to pull a payback prank. After all, the valets had poured the drinks at dinner last night.

The household staff was loyal to the first family, but what would they do if Zora and Sky asked them for help?

Which first family would they choose?

Loyalty counted, but so did the years ahead. The household staff would literally have to live with Zora and Skylar for at least four more years, eight if things went well for the new president and the country.

And Ingrid and Winnie? In a few weeks, they'd be history.

"Hi, Ingrid," Kate said, back for her morning shift.

Ingrid was happy to find a friendly face. "Hi, Kate. Are you having a good morning?"

"The best," Kate said, and placed Ingrid's favorite breakfast on the table: pancakes and orange juice.

"Wow!" Ingrid said. "You've outdone yourself. Thank you!"

This morning, the pancakes were decorated with snow-flakes made out of cream and powdered sugar.

A thought popped into Ingrid's mind, and she eyed her plate with distrust.

Kate ruffled Ingrid's hair. "It's totally safe. I heard about last night's prank, but we in the upstairs kitchen don't mess up with the food, I promise."

A few years back, Ingrid and the whole household had had a scare when her oatmeal had been cross-contaminated with wheat. Ingrid had a terrible allergic reaction to the gluten, and ever since, the cooks had been extra careful with her meals even though she'd outgrown her food sensitivities. She still remembered the panic as her throat closed up and she couldn't breathe. Good thing Winnie had run out to ask for help, and good thing Kate carried an EpiPen because she had a nut allergy. She had saved Ingrid, who'd never forgotten how a simple mouthful of a favorite food could become deadly.

"I know, Kate. It's just that . . . it feels different here with another family." She took a bite of pancake and chased it with OJ.

Kate laughed. "So the honeymoon lasted less than twenty-four hours? A lot of us were wondering how long until you girls had a falling-out, but no one guessed it would be so soon!"

Ingrid was horrified. "It's not a falling-out, Kate. We're all still friends. I promise."

Kate looked doubtful, but she nodded. "I hope so. We love all of you girls the same."

The words were supposed to be comforting, but Ingrid's heart twanged. The staff loved them all *the same*?

"Did they say something about Winnie and me?" Ingrid asked. "I promise my sister and I never imagined an ice cube would create such a panic."

Kate wrote something in the notebook where she kept track of things to order and said, "I believe you, Ingrid. Still, I feel bad for the Williams girls. We all just want the four of you to get along. You know, a lot of people will be waiting for any kind of drama to give free rein to their gossip."

Kate went back to her work while Ingrid finished her breakfast and continued with her before-school chores—unloading one of the dishwashers—deep in thought. She had to tell Winnie that the staff was worried about the four of them not being friends anymore.

While she worked, two of the cooks, Martha and Ray, were muttering under their breath and opening and closing drawers with a bit of frustration.

"What's going on?" Ingrid asked.

"We can't find the plastic wrap," Ray said.

Martha looked at Ingrid. "Did you and your sister take out the plastic wrap to play a prank on the Williams sisters?"

Ingrid's cheeks flamed, thinking that her reaction might make her look guilty of something she hadn't done. "No! We . . . that is to say, I . . . promised my mom that last night's prank was it. It didn't even qualify as a prank, but everyone keeps calling it that." A horrible feeling crept inside her. "Why? What happened?"

Winnie popped into the kitchen just then. As if she could sense the tension, she said, "Whatever it is, I didn't do it. I promise."

Martha huffed, frustrated, and kept looking inside the cupboards.

"All the plastic-wrap tubes are gone," Ray said, his eyes big with the same surprise Ingrid felt. Things had never gone missing in the kitchen before, as far as she knew.

"All of them?" Winnie asked, a look of suspicion on her face.

"All of them," said Martha. "I checked on the third-floor kitchenette, and I couldn't find any plastic wrap there, either."

"Maybe we ran out?" Ingrid said, knowing perfectly well that was impossible. The house staff was always on top of ordering everything needed to run the household as smoothly as possible. Ingrid had even seen a YouTube video that claimed that the White House had a secret warehouse underground.

Ridiculous!

There was no mystery or magic involved—just the extreme competence of the staff. They always stocked up well in advance so that no essential item would ever run out. From the girls' favorite snacks to toilet paper, garbage bags, and even First Ferret Lafayette's favorite treats, whatever they needed was always at hand in a closet, pantry, or storage room. Just before the Williams girls' arrival, Mami had been double-checking the supplies. She'd have noticed if the plastic wrap had disappeared from every kitchen.

"It's okay," Kate said, paper in hand. "I know we got the usual grocery order yesterday, but maybe it wasn't all delivered? Or maybe the new rolls were misplaced?"

"Maybe," said Ray, sounding more hopeful than certain. Because of security reasons, the White House didn't receive any direct store deliveries. Instead, things were sent to other buildings and then transported to the White

House. With so many stops along the way, it was possible for things to get lost in transit.

It had just never happened before.

"But what about the ones we already had?" Winnie asked. "Even if the delivery didn't arrive, it's not like we were all out before, right?" She'd been helping the kitchen staff a few days ago, so she would know if something was missing.

Ray just shrugged.

The day ahead would be another busy one in the house. Kate and Martha went back to work, while Ray made a run to a store a couple of blocks away for some plastic wrap.

Winnie helped Ingrid finish putting the last cups away where they belonged, and then they walked just outside the kitchen to put their thoughts in order.

"They took the plastic wrap!" Ingrid said, breathless with excitement.

"But why?" Winnie replied.

"I bet anything they're going to use it to prank us. But what can they do with plastic wrap, though?" asked Ingrid, her mind rushing a mile a minute over every possibility. She couldn't come up with anything.

"I don't know," Winnie replied. "But I'm going to find out. Now, act natural. I hear them coming."

Ingrid heard the twins chatting with one of the ushers, Robert.

"After I apologize, again, like I promised Mami, I'm going to ask them if they're behind this," Ingrid said.

Ingrid had promised Mami that there would be peace in the household. Besides, the whole staff was looking at them to see if it was true that the girls had had a falling-out, and it was better to tell the other girls about the expectations for first daughters face-to-face. But Winnie looked at her with shiny eyes. Her face was the epitome of mischievous.

Ingrid hadn't seen her sister so excited about anything in a long time.

"What?" she asked.

"It's just that if the Williams twins do strike back, then who can blame us for returning the prank? We just won't let anyone else know. Imagine what they'd say about us in the history books? Think about the jokes you'll be able to tell, Ingrid! We need to discover what they're scheming."

WINNIE

It felt like ages had passed after the dinner fiasco, but Winnie had finally heard back from Javi Rojas.

"Ingrid!" She called her sister, who was coming back from piano lessons in the Music Room. "You need to hear this!"

Ingrid ran to her side, and together they hit the gym, which was empty in the afternoon.

"What did he say?" Ingrid asked. "Does he hate us?"

Winnie stepped back to look at her and scoffed. "Of course not! He's not upset at Zora and Skylar either. He just asked if he can come over to interview us."

"When? What for?"

"As soon as possible. And what do you mean, what for?

The piece he's writing for *Verified Teen*. His article is being published right after Inauguration Day!" Winnie said, grabbing a five-pound weight and doing bicep curls. "He says he wants to show our version of what it's like to be a kid in the White House."

"Well," Ingrid said, "Zora and Skylar are not even officially moved in yet. Our opinion is the one that counts the most, don't you think?"

Winnie shook her head and put the weight down on the rack. "Ingrid, are you really that jealous of them because they're staying here after January?"

Ingrid grabbed a jump rope and twisted it in her hands. "Not jealous," she said with a wistful expression on her face. "It's just that the last joke I posted didn't have as many comments as usual. People will forget all about me when we're gone."

"Well, this piece Javi is writing will prove we're the coolest ones, no matter what silly polls say. Now, let's go see if we can find the plastic wrap and prove they're planning a prank of their own."

Ingrid put the jump rope back on its hook and followed her sister out to the hallway. "Where are they now anyway? They never want to hang out. They're busier than us!"

"At etiquette class," Winnie said. "I saw them heading to the East Room. Now, let's check behind the Christmas trees."

"Why the trees?"

Winnie narrowed her eyes. "I have a hunch. Besides, this morning, Santiago found an empty cardboard roll behind the Gold Star Christmas tree."

The Gold Star was the one honoring the families who'd lost loved ones serving in the armed forces.

"He did?" Ingrid asked, peeking behind the tree decorated with flags from every country in the world.

"He totally did."

They spent the next few minutes searching behind the differently themed trees along the Center Hall. There were so many. One for Papi's favorite beverage besides coffee, Jarritos; one dedicated to national sports teams; one built out of Mami's favorite picture books; a magazine tree; even one dedicated to Laffy.

"It breaks my heart that they hate Laffy because of the ice cubes," Winnie said, gazing at her favorite ornament, one with her ferret photoshopped into a tuxedo. "It's not like he did anything, poor thing."

"I know," Ingrid replied. "We can't let his fan club find out they don't like him, though. Ferret people are . . . intense." Then she exclaimed, "Oh! Look at this, Win!"

"What?" she asked, running to her sister's side. "Did you find anything?"

Ingrid showed her an old ornament with a picture of the two of them in red-and-white elf outfits. "Aw," she said, and the softness of her own voice surprised her. "I remember that day. We were so happy, helping Santa pass out presents to every member of the staff."

Ingrid rested her chin on Winnie's shoulder. "Yes, we were."

Surprisingly, Winnie felt a twinge of regret that next year, she wouldn't be here to make new Christmas memories.

"Girls! Where are you?" Alice called from the end of the hallway.

Winnie looked at her watch and flinched. "Yikes. I forgot! The *Nutcracker* performance in the Library. Let's go before we get in trouble."

And they ran to join their mom and their guests.

A few days later, Ingrid found a cardboard roll behind the Latin American–themed tree in the flower shop.

"Winnie, is this a plastic–wrap roll?"

Winnie looked at it, but then Kate told them it was actually from a roll of gift-wrapping paper that the decorators must have left behind. Worse, it matched the one Santiago had found.

"I guess that ends the theory that the previous roll belonged to the missing plastic wrap," Winnie said.

"Maybe they really had nothing to do with it, Win," Ingrid said as they headed to school.

"Maybe," Winnie said, shrugging. But something told her Zora and Skylar were behind the mystery.

She really didn't have any proof that the Williams girls had taken the plastic wrap, but she had hoped the Williams sisters would prank the two of them back. It would've been so fun! Even if they'd sent one of their mom's aides instead of doing it themselves, the responsibility for the prank was still on them. With so many new faces around the house, Ingrid and Winnie didn't know who to trust other than the people they'd known since they were little.

She had no idea what the Williams girls would plan to do with all the plastic, so when they got home, Winnie went online, searching for pranking tips. She was horrified at what she discovered.

"Placing plastic on doorways? On top of toilets?" Winnie exclaimed after reading a random article about pranks college seniors played on freshmen. As she had expected, Ingrid was in shock at what she heard.

"Why would they do that? I mean, putting plastic on the toilets," Ingrid said.

Winnie rolled her eyes. "Really, Ingrid? Think about it. To have some fun! They know we wouldn't go to Mami and Papi with the gossip. In their eyes, we'd be even."

"But wouldn't we?"

Winnie's eyes flashed. "No! This is still *our* house, and I refuse to be worried about what toilet I use or getting stuck in my doorway like a bug in a spiderweb."

Until she said it aloud, she hadn't recognized this was what she felt.

This was her house.

Not forever, but for now.

"It's still all speculation, Win. We don't know they'll prank us like that, do we?" Ingrid said as they headed downstairs for some free time.

Winnie didn't have time to reply. When they reached the ground floor, they came face-to-face with the Williams girls, who were walking upstairs.

"Hey!" she said, hoping she and Ingrid didn't look like they were gossiping about them.

"Hey, we were looking for you. Do you want to go bowling for an hour or so?" Skylar asked. Zora fidgeted, a book under her arm.

Ingrid and Winnie looked at each other and beamed.

"Sure!" Ingrid said.

"I haven't been forever," Winnie replied. If the Williamses were going to prank her and her sister, it was better to keep a close eye on them.

The four girls walked together to the basement, where the one-lane bowling alley was, following the signs indicating TRUMAN BOWLING ALLEY. When they reached the hallway with the black and white checkered tiles, Winnie said, "Look. I always do this. Only jump on the black tiles." She hopscotched until she came to another circular staircase that was carpeted in moss green. Behind her, Ingrid, Skylar, and Zora hopscotched until they reached her.

They laughed as they struggled to jump on one foot, and rosy-cheeked and a little out of breath, they kept going.

"Wow," said Zora, her eyes wide, when they reached a hallway with cement floors and exposed ducts overhead. "It really is the basement. Underneath where exactly are we?"

"The portico," Ingrid said. "Isn't it cool?"

"I hope there's no bugs down here," Skylar said, and Winnie was happy she was leading the way so no one else could see her roll her eyes. Of course there had to be some kind of bug. It was a basement, after all.

She stopped in front of a door with the number 037, and underneath, TRUMAN BOWLING ALLEY in gold letters. "Here we are."

"It's not the actual Truman lanes," Zora said in her know-it-all voice. "That was in the executive building across the street. The Eisenhower was originally built for the State, War, and Navy Departments. . . ."

Winnie winked at Ingrid and went ahead to turn the lights on. At the sight of an impressive mounted cabinet with immaculate white leather bowling shoes in all sizes, Zora's voice trailed off.

"This is amazing!" Skylar exclaimed as she took a pair of shoes and examined them.

"Those are my mom's. See her initials? PMBP for Paloma Mabel Bianchi López," Ingrid said. "But the ones on the right are all unworn shoes for guests. Don't look so sad, Skylar. I'm sure the ones engraved with your initials will be here on Inauguration Day. What's your shoe size?"

Winnie handed Zora a pair in her size, and once they had changed, they picked their balls. "This one has my initials, but you can borrow it if you want neon pink," Winnie said, feeling generous with Skylar.

Skylar narrowed her eyes. "Why do you assume my favorite color is pink?"

Again, the electricity between the pairs of sisters sizzled, until Skylar laughed. "Got you! My favorite color *is* pink!"

Winnie smiled. "I knew it!" She handed Skylar the pink ball, and she played with her mom's turquoise one. Ingrid grabbed green, and Zora a sparkly silver one.

"Oh!" Ingrid said. "You never cease to surprise us, Zora!"

Winnie was the first one to go. She stood in front of the lane, brought the ball to just below her chin, and calculated. She took one, two steps, slid her right foot behind the left one gracefully, like she was rehearsing a dance, swung her arm, and let the ball go.

She held her breath as the ball slid toward the line of pins and struck it perfectly.

"Come on, come on," she muttered as the final pin wobbled.

When it finally collapsed, she raised her arms in the air. "Yes!"

Ingrid jumped to hug her.

"How did you do that?" Skylar asked.

Winnie loved competing. She lived for winning. But surprisingly, she also loved the challenge of teaching.

"To throw the perfect curve ball, this is what you do."

They practiced for the next few minutes until all four of them were getting strike after strike. They were having so much fun, Winnie forgot about teams, and points, and winning.

Finally, things between them seemed like back on the campaign trail, during the rare moments they could sneak away from the grown-ups and their seriousness and just be friends.

They were laughing at Ingrid trying to walk along the lane and slipping. Zora and Skylar were sprawled on the neon-green and red leather chairs, and Winnie sat against the wall where the photos of Presidents Bush and Obama playing were hung.

When Kate opened the door, the four froze, although

they were doing nothing wrong.

"Don't stop laughing. I brought you some pizzas, girls," she said, and placed them on the counter at the back of the room.

"Thanks, Kate! We love you!" Winnie said.

"We love you!" the other three girls cried.

Kate smiled. "I love getting to see the four of you like this. I wish I could snap a picture."

And Winnie realized that she too wished she could remember this moment forever. It was the most fun she'd had in ages. And all because she'd finally given the Williams sisters a fair chance.

Later that night in her room, Ingrid was braiding Winnie's hair and said, "Maybe the plastic wrap wasn't them after all. And if it was, I'm sure nothing will come of it."

Winnie nodded. "I think you're right." She looked at her sister over her shoulder. "Now, Ingrid, do *The Nutcracker* one more time before bed."

And Ingrid complied, imitating one of the scenes from the production of *The Nutcracker* they'd seen a few days before. She did a mean Rat King. Winnie laughed until she got tears in her eyes.

A week after the Williams girls had moved in, when Winnie was on her way back to the second floor after her piano lesson, Mami asked, "Where are you going, Win?"

Winnie smiled charmingly and said, "My bathroom, Mami."

"Why do you only use the one in your room? Is something wrong with the one upstairs?"

Winnie had lowered her defenses about the Williams girls, but she still only liked to use her own bathroom. Just in case.

"I just like mine better. That's all," she said.

"I never knew you were so particular," Mami said.

"We all have our quirks," said Winnie with a grin, and then she said what had really been on her mind. "Besides, the house feels a little different with the Williamses here, you know."

Mami had a pensive look in her eye.

"What?" Winnie urged, like a chismosa, a typical gossiper. "You feel the same way?"

Her mom would never say anything negative about another person, much less about special guests, but before she denied Winnie's suspicions, the sounds of strange voices announced a group of people who were heading to the third floor.

Winnie waited until they were gone to say, "There are so many people in the house."

Although the White House consisted of almost 55,000 square feet of floor space, it was starting to feel a little too tight for comfort. At least for Winnie. She imagined it couldn't be easy for Mami either.

"The Williamses and their staff are perfect guests," Mami said. "It's those who don't even step inside the house who make me anxious sometimes."

Winnie knew exactly what she was talking about. This morning during breakfast, the news anchor on TV had reported that Zora and Skylar weren't attending the same school as Winnie and Ingrid. The tabloids were having a field day speculating that there was trouble in the White House, even though this had been public knowledge since day one. Even Javi had texted Winnie to ask if it was true.

It was obvious the rumors were starting to get to Mami too. Being in charge of managing both households until Mr. Williams got his feet under him couldn't be easy.

"Come on . . . tell me," she urged Mami.

Mami laughed. "Before I say something I'll regret later, let me go back to work. I'm determined to finish signing the interminable stack of thank-you notes on my desk."

"But you've been at it for weeks, Mami." Winnie's face burned when she remembered the stack of cards she and Ingrid had yet to send to their friends so they'd know their new address. She'd ask Leo for help the next time she saw him.

Mami sighed and shook her hand as if it hurt. "I. Know. But the last eight years wouldn't have been possible without a lot of help from a whole lot of people. You know?

Especially those who helped take care of your sister and you. You, mainly."

Winnie struck an angelic pose, clasping her hands under her chin. Then, before her mom could get started on all the nannies who'd come and gone through the years, unable to keep up with her antics, she continued toward her room while Mami went on to her office.

Most of the nannies had been wonderful, but she was glad they didn't have them anymore. Otherwise, she and Ingrid never would've had any fun.

As if thoughts of nannies had called Agent Sisco, when she turned into her hallway, she heard his voice as he spoke into his headset. "The coast is clear," he muttered. "Lafayette is moved, and Popcorn is nowhere to be seen."

Winnie jumped out of his way before they crashed.

"Oof, sorry, Pop—I mean, Win," he said. Poor Sisco. His forehead was crisscrossed with worry lines. She didn't even have the heart to be offended that he'd called her Popcorn. "I didn't see you," he said, flustered. After all, it was his job to see everything. Especially when it came to the girls.

"It's all good. I was just heading to my room," she said, patting his arm, which was like patting a steel bar.

He pressed his lips and shook his head. "Unfortunately, your room is out of bounds for you."

Winnie felt a wave of dread rising inside her. "What?

Why?" She went through her actions earlier in the morning. Had she forgotten to turn off the sink again?

"Nothing bad happened," he hurried to explain. "But there's a decorator and his team taking measurements in there, and you can't be around, for your own safety."

"But I . . . I have to go."

"Sorry, Win. You're going to have to use the one in the hallway. Like I said, there's a group of people drawing all kinds of plans in there now," Sisco said.

Horror gripped Winnie.

"Plans for what?" she asked, appalled.

"That will be Skylar's room when your family moves out."

"But it's still *my* room," she said.

Agent Sisco was obviously trying to make an effort not to laugh. Why did he think this was funny? "It is a perfect opportunity, if you think about it."

"In the past, that's all been done after the current family moves out," she said.

Sisco nodded. "True, but I assure you the household will be grateful for all the help they can get before the move. Besides, Mr. Williams asked, very politely, I might add, if there was a way the decorator could take a look," he said. "Your mom said it was okay."

Smart of Sisco to add this. He knew Winnie wouldn't complain—too much—if Mami had said it was okay.

"But why today? I just saw my mom, and she didn't tell me anything about it."

"Because you were supposed to be at piano lessons for another half hour," he said, looking at his watch. "And your mom wasn't sure when the decorators would get clearance again after today."

Winnie sighed and rolled her eyes.

"I'll go to Ingrid's. She won't mind I'm in her room for a little while."

Sisco shook his head. "Sorry, Win, you can't be in this wing at all. Not while the decorator and his crew are there. Too much of a security threat."

She hated to be treated like a fragile princess. What could happen to her in her own house? But the decorators were doing their job. Agent Sisco was doing his job too. Winnie didn't like putting everyone out of their way as if she was a diva.

"Go back to the third floor," he said. "You can say hi to Laffy. He's up there for now."

"You moved him?" she asked, outraged and a little worried.

Sisco walked her down the hallway toward the back stairs that led to the Linen Room. "He's right off the Greenhouse. He looked happy getting some sunshine."

"He gets sunshine from my window, Sisco," she said.

Agent Sisco's mouth twitched like when he was trying

not to smile. "Go say hi to him. You can use that bathroom across from the staircase. Now, go on. Don't get lost."

She stomped all the way to the third floor, each step an exclamation point.

She stopped in her tracks when she saw First Ferret Lafayette's cage in the hallway that led to the Greenhouse, like Sisco had said. Even though she'd cleaned the cage, she could still smell his musky scent.

What had the decorator and Mr. Williams thought about Laffy? Had the smell from his cage lingered? Winnie went into the bathroom, fuming that she couldn't even go into her own room. When she was about to come out, she heard footsteps in the hallway. She waited, not wanting to come face to face with anyone from the Williamses' crew. By the time she finally decided it was safe to head back to the Music Room, she was so mad that she slammed the door a little harder than she'd intended.

A horrible noise, like a mix of a duck in pain and a moose trumpeting, blared throughout the hallway and made her jump three feet in the air. Her flailing arms made contact with an accent table that she would swear hadn't been there a few minutes ago, and when it fell, it took down a big decorative vase filled with holiday flowers.

She launched herself to catch it before it fell on the floor and shattered. The vase looked expensive and old, like everything else in the house. Anything that broke would have to be replaced and paid for by Papi, and she'd already gotten an earful for ordering chocolate cake more than usual this last month. Her fingers barely grazed the blue-and-white ceramic vase, which landed with an ominous clank and crack. The little table tottered and fell on her head, along with a pile of thin rectangular boxes that had been hidden behind the vase.

Her head throbbed, but her first thought was: *The missing plastic wrap!*

"I knew it!" she said, and scrambled to get up in case someone was around and saw her on the floor.

When she thought the worst was over, she leaned against the bathroom door, and the honking sound startled her again. She looked up and saw a toy cornet thingie on top of the door hinge.

Those girls!

They must have planted the booby trap when she went into the bathroom!

Winnie's ears rang with a mixture of feelings she didn't know how to name. She'd been bested. In her own house! But she also felt triumphant that the Williams girls had risen to the challenge and pranked her back. She didn't have much time to savor all the feelings, because the stomping sound of feet running in her direction came closer, along with the sound of girlish giggles following close behind.

The first one to reach her was Agent Sisco, who was

red-faced as he ran in her direction, closely followed by Skylar and Zora.

He had seen her in all her looks, states of mind, and levels of grounding. Any self-consciousness Winnie might have felt when it came to him and the rest of the Secret Service officers had been lost long, long ago. But the Williams sisters! She couldn't let them see how she felt about being defeated at her own game.

In a move that would have impressed Mr. Williams, the actor, Winnie trained her face into the coolest, fakest smile she could muster and turned toward them. Instead, a young woman Winnie had never seen before chose that specific moment to peek out from the Greenhouse into the hallway. "Everything okay out here?" she asked.

Agent Sisco tried to skid to a stop so he wouldn't crash into the mountain of cardboard boxes and broken pieces of vase. He was like a meteor headed for Planet Earth with the potential to obliterate all civilizations. Typical Sisco. But when he changed direction abruptly to avoid colliding with the woman, he rammed straight into Lafayette's cage.

Laffy squeaked in terror. Poor thing! He wasn't usually allowed out of Winnie's room, the house being a museum and all. This had to be the most excitement he'd had in his whole life.

"I'm sorry!" the woman said, her eyes wide at the sight of the mess in front of her.

"Are you okay, Win?" Sisco asked. Then he turned to the woman and glowered at her. "And who are you?"

The lady's cheeks blazed as she waved a visitor's badge in his face. "I'm part of the decorator group, Agent Sisco. Remember me? Mrs. López allowed me to look at plant options for Skylar's room in the Greenhouse."

Agent Sisco scratched his head in apparent embarrassment at his overreaction and spoke into his earpiece. "Everything okay. We'll just need housekeeping for a minor . . . incident." When he saw the boxes of plastic wrap on the floor, he muttered, "Oh! That's where I left them! Nelson's gonna give me an earful!"

Winnie gasped.

Agent Sisco turned to look at her and his cheeks turned bright red.

Winnie exclaimed, "You lost the plastic wrap! We thought it had been the twins!"

"Why?" he asked. "And what's all this mess?"

"What mess?" she asked, placing a hand over her still-racing heart. "I didn't do anything."

He made a sweeping motion at the destruction in the hallway like he was presenting evidence against her.

"Ask *them!*" Winnie pointed at Zora and Skylar, who were muttering at each other.

"Us?" Zora asked while Skylar made her innocent-little-lamb face.

"Winnie," Sisco said with a warning tone in his voice. "Please don't raise your voice."

She rounded on him. "I'm not raising my voice!"

In that moment, Papi joined them in the hallway, followed by Ingrid and President-Elect Williams.

"What happened?" Papi asked, sounding a little worried and very disappointed. He was always so strict about respect, and now that she'd snapped out of it, Winnie realized she *had* been raising her voice.

"I didn't know you were on this floor," Winnie said. Had she known her papi and Mrs. Williams were in a meeting on the third floor, she'd have headed to the first-floor bathroom, or to her mom's office. She was rambunctious, but she'd never interfered with presidential business.

Now she never got the chance to explain. Ingrid took charge.

"Oh," she said, "I see Winnie went looking for the missing plastic wrap and found it. We didn't tell you, Papi, but all the plastic wrap in the house went missing a few days ago, so we've been trying to solve the mystery." She took a breath, and Winnie made a signal for her to stop divulging the details of their quest. Even Zora conspicuously elbowed Ingrid, who just couldn't take the hint as she went on.

By now, Mami and Mr. Williams had also joined them, alerted by either the horn, Winnie's shriek, the sound of the vase breaking, the running feet, or all of the above.

Her face went through all the shades of red Winnie had seen in her life as a troublemaker and a few she didn't think her mom could pull, given her skin tone and her makeup.

Papi and Mr. Williams looked like they were trying not to laugh, but President-Elect Williams obviously disapproved of the whole situation. Her mouth was a straight line. Winnie didn't dare to ad-lib.

"So, judging by all the boxes of plastic wrap, I assume Winnie finally found them. Then that loud sound we heard must have scared her, and somehow she demolished that vase. That's all I have," Ingrid said, looking at Winnie and the other girls as if asking for the extra details that no one would be self-destructive enough to provide.

Papi, not only the president of the country but also the head of the household they all lived in, cleared his throat and said, "I love that you girls are having fun. Friendly pranks are a great tradition. . . . By the way, Theresa, watch out for those missing keyboard letters, but don't let my staff know I said anything, okay?"

The adults, including the decorator and Agent Sisco, laughed politely, but Paloma gently elbowed him. Never before had Winnie seen the resemblance between Papi and Ingrid more clearly than at this moment.

"Now that you all had your fun doing a treasure hunt," he continued, "I think everyone—from the families to the staff—will be happy if this is the end of it." He sent Winnie and Ingrid a pointed look that meant the discussion was over for now, but more would be coming later.

"Help your sister pick this up, Ingrid," Mami said.

"It's not fair—" Winnie said, and a look from her mom stopped her just in time.

President-Elect Williams added, "Zora and Sky, please help too."

"Oh no, Theresa, please," Mami said, placing a hand on Mrs. Williams's arm. Looking at the twins, she added, "You're guests here, girls. Besides, the extra work won't hurt my daughters. Believe me."

Winnie clenched her teeth so she wouldn't talk back to her mom in front of *the guests*.

One by one, the adults, including Agent Sisco, left.

On her way back to the greenhouse, the decorator lady glanced at Winnie in such an offended way, as if she hadn't been the one who had caused the whole problem! If she hadn't stepped out of the Greenhouse at the wrong moment, Agent Sisco wouldn't have bumped into Laffy's cage, and the whole White House wouldn't have come to investigate what had happened. Winnie had had the situation under control until the lady ruined everything.

"What are all those people doing in my room anyway?" Winnie asked, picking up a piece of the broken vase.

Skylar and Zora were righting the toppled table.

"The decorator wants to change the paint color," Skylar said. "She says that's a horrible shade of blue."

Winnie was livid. "Nice of you to say that. I originally wanted the walls painted pink, but when I found out I wouldn't be allowed to open the windows, I went with sky blue." A knot grew in her throat when she remembered how little she'd been when she'd first moved into this house. She swallowed and tried to shake the cloud of sadness inching closer and closer to her. When they were at the new California house, she'd paint her walls like a rainbow, and she would never have to worry about asking permission from a curator.

"I said I wanted to keep the blue, though," Skylar said in a small voice.

Winnie's heart softened in spite of herself.

"And I wanted to preserve the historic nature of the house, so I'm okay with the cream color, Ingrid," Zora added, flicking her wrist like the decision was obvious.

"Sorry about the vase," Skylar said. "We didn't mean for the horn to scare you—that much."

"So it *was* you," Winnie said with a delighted gasp, but the twins had already left.

Everything had been picked up. The only casualties were the vase and Winnie's pride.

Ingrid looked at Winnie and shrugged like Elmo. "Oh, well."

"That was a good one. The horn almost killed me," Winnie said, studying the back of the bathroom door to see how in the world the twins had managed to wedge in a horn that would blare so loudly with the right pressure. "See? I was right about them planning something. I just didn't know what it was."

Ingrid was uncharacteristically quiet. Winnie turned to see if she had left too. But Ingrid was still there, staring at Laffy's cage.

It wasn't the expression on Ingrid's face that made the hairs rise on the back of Winnie's neck, but the fact that Ingrid seemed to be at a loss for words. She was pointing at something, openmouthed.

Winnie followed the direction of Ingrid's finger, but she couldn't understand what her sister was trying to say. Her first thought was that she'd made a hole in the wall or ruined something else.

"What?" she asked.

"Laffy," Ingrid said in a choked voice.

Winnie squinted her eyes. The lighting in this hallway was horrible! "What, Ingrid! Spit it out! I don't see . . ." Her words trailed off. She didn't see . . . Laffy, that was, which was exactly the issue.

"Where is he?" Ingrid asked.

There was no sign of the first ferret.

Winnie inspected the cage, but it was definitely empty,

the side door depressingly ajar.

"In all the ruckus, the door must have gotten unlocked . . . ," Ingrid said.

Winnie shook her head. The door had always been a little iffy, and she had secured that side of the cage against the wall in her room to prevent something like this happening. If only the person who had moved the cage had been more careful!

"Laffy's gone," she said, her dark eyes boring into her sister's. "Even if they didn't mean to do it, this means war."

She took out her phone and texted Javi.

ZORA

Zora didn't want that boy, Javi, interviewing her for a magazine article. For *Verified Teen* even less. Not because she didn't like the publication. In fact, it was the only teen magazine she subscribed to. During the last few years, it had reported on everything from health to politics with an honesty and professionalism other magazines had ditched in the name of not offending big names. She respected *Verified Teen*.

And it wasn't that she didn't like Javi, either. He was cute and smart. And kind. But after a few weeks at the White House, she couldn't wait for things to settle down. And this was too much.

"All my underwear is gone!" She kicked at the precarious

heap of packing boxes, and the pile of books she'd borrowed from the Library downstairs toppled to the floor.

Fortunately, she and Skylar had an unspoken system going. Only one of them was allowed to lose it at a time. They'd never set up this system; it had just happened. Maybe it was a twin thing.

Skylar placed a hand on Zora's shoulder and pulled her close for a hug. Zora hadn't been expecting the gesture, but she leaned into her sister and took a deep breath.

"You're okay, darling," Skylar said in a pretend British accent that made Zora laugh.

She was so grateful that she had her sister and didn't have to go through this whole first-daughter experience by herself.

"Tell me," Skylar said, "why are you freaking out, Zora Jo 'Thunder' Williams?"

Zora looked even more miserable. Her chin quivered.

"They couldn't have chosen a more ridiculous name?" Zora asked. *They* was the Secret Service. "Are they making fun of me? They named you Twinkle. It matches you. But why name me *Thunder*?" She bellowed in her own way, which wasn't loud at all.

"Oh, Zora, what's really going on?" Skylar said.

Zora shrugged. How could she explain without sounding like she was making a mountain out of a speck of dust?

Her missing underwear more than qualified as a first-world problem, but it was like that little drop that makes the whole cup spill.

Skylar must have known that Zora wasn't ready to express what was bothering her yet, so she changed tactics. "Remember Winnie's face when she figured out about the plastic-wrap rolls?" She bit her lip and smiled devilishly.

Zora, who'd been about to cry, snorted, and the sound made her laugh. Soon both of them were laughing and laughing, and like magic, the rising tension inside Zora stopped pressing so hard.

"That was epic," she said. "But do you think we crossed a line? She and Ingrid didn't look happy when their dad told them to stop the pranks."

"No, they didn't," Skylar said, cringing. "But he didn't sound very angry, either. It was hilarious to hear that horn and then Winnie's scream, though." She giggled at the memory. "The one who looked angrier was that agent, Sisco. He's so serious. It was just a joke."

"And the poor ferret," Zora said, picturing the worst-case scenario her mind could come up with, because that was her specialty. A loose ferret could cause a lot of trouble in the White House. She was afraid there wouldn't be a happy ending for him. "They need to find him soon. Mrs. López told Dad almost a hundred thousand people come through the house for the holidays. . . ."

Zora could see this information had shocked Skylar, because her sister's face paled for a second. "One hundred thousand visitors at the house we live at?"

"The house we're guests at right now. There's a big difference, Sky. Even Mrs. López said so."

Skylar sighed.

"If he didn't escape, with so many nooks and crannies in this house, he could be anywhere. Remember the unfinished parts of the basement we saw on the way to the bowling alley?" Zora said, rubbing her chin and thinking of the other stuff that could be lost, or hidden.

Infuriatingly embarrassing stuff, like her underwear.

As if she'd guessed what Zora was thinking, Skylar said, "You could ask Dad or one of the assistants to order you new underwear."

Zora sighed and nodded. "It can't be that hard to move my clothes from our old house to my new room. The boxes had my name in bright pink Sharpie. I mean . . . you got yours without a problem. Why did mine get lost?"

"Maybe it got mixed with other stuff. Agent Lee said she was looking, but there were too many similar boxes in one of the subbasements. You saw that the basement is a total maze. Imagine what the subbasements are like!"

Agent Lee had taken on the task of finding the missing

box personally, without results, which didn't help Zora feel any better.

"It would also be easy for anyone to take it knowing it was yours," Skylar said, adding to her misgivings. "But this is an opportunity to get new stuff, Z! Look at it that way."

Zora rolled her eyes and groaned. Sometimes Skylar just didn't get it. She didn't understand how Zora wanted her own things just the way they always were, to help her feel better and at home. She flopped onto her bed and turned on the lamp on the nightstand. It was getting dark.

"Girls!" Their dad's voice sounded from the hallway this time, making both of them jump. "Time to go. The stylists are here!"

"Stylists!" Zora and Skylar both exclaimed, although the tones of their voices and the expressions on their faces couldn't have been more different.

Skylar's eyes sparkled like jewels. Her smile brightened the room, making up for the gray clouds outside the window. She'd been searching for a dress for Inauguration Day since their mom had announced she was running for the presidency two years ago.

For her part, Zora felt like she was going to die if she had to go through another catalog of expensive, uncomfortable clothes that she wouldn't be allowed to keep, much less wear more than once.

If she could have let Skylar choose sensible, comfy clothes for them, she wouldn't have been so upset. How did Winnie and Ingrid deal with needing to look like dolls 24/7? Maybe they didn't know any better? Maybe because they'd never tasted freedom like Zora and her sister had? She hoped that after the holidays, the pressure to be social would lessen a bit.

"I kind of wanted to read a book I found in the Library," she said, with as much sentiment as she could afford without sounding bratty. "I'm already tired from just planning all the parties. Imagine the parties themselves."

Skylar made a face. "Remember what Mom said. Being social is the least we can do as first daughters. And we can show the world we're doing a better job at it than the López girls."

"How?" Zora asked, sitting on her bed.

Skylar beamed at her. "In that interview thing Javi Rojas is working on. Did you remember to send him pictures from our birthdays?"

Zora rolled her eyes. "Of course."

"And you sent him the best ones? Did you figure out how to access them in the cloud?"

She jumped to her feet and, crossing her arms, asked, "Of course! Did you forget who you're talking to? I sent him the best collection of photos to show that we, the Williams girls, have been *slaying* at this first-daughter business since before we were born."

"You're the best," Skylar said.

Someone knocked on the door.

"Come in," Zora said.

Annie, one of the aides, popped in and announced, "Are you girls ready?"

"Yes!" Skylar replied, jumping from the bed.

"I guess," said Zora. She followed her sister to what had once been called the Empire Room and now was an office that had been yielded to their father. The desks were gleaming, and antique lamps she'd helped him choose from a catalog lit up the room. The scent of Dad's favorite sage-and-bergamot candle reminded her of home. Her real home in Baltimore.

Their father smiled at them. "Hello, darlings," he said. "I love to see your happy faces."

Zora made an effort to smile widely, and surprisingly, she felt a small twinge of comfort. As long as she was measuring up to the task of being a good helper for her mom, a good team member in their family, she felt okay.

"Here are the preliminary outfits for the upcoming events," Annie said, pointing at two racks of clothes. "This is yours, Sky." She pointed at the one with all the cashmere sweaters and frilly dresses. There was even a hook for hair accessories. "And that one's yours, Zora," Annie said, but she looked at Skylar.

"I'm Zora." She walked up to the rack and went through the outfits.

"Let's try them on," Skylar said.

"I'm not changing here!" Zora crossed her arms as if her sister had tried to take her sweater off.

Annie laughed. "Of course not here! Look, Zora, the adjacent room has been set up with full body mirrors. Charlotte is bringing more dresses just in case."

"Can I just have Sky choose for me?"

Sky shook her head. "Come on, I'll help you."

Together with Annie, they wheeled the racks into the next room.

"Let me know if you need anything. I'll be right here," Annie said before softly closing the door.

Skylar took out something from Zora's rack.

"That's my pile," she said, but Skylar was already handing her the hanger with a silk shift dress. "Try this on."

Zora obliged while Skylar told Zora the history of silk and different dyeing techniques, and what the best styles were for every person's body type. She knew how to make fashion appeal to Zora's nerdy heart.

"Silk is delicate, and yet a strand is stronger than steel," she said, brushing her fingers on an exquisite champagne-colored dress. "Historically, it's also been used as money."

"Currency, you mean?"

Skylar grinned. "Yes, currency! And guess what!"

"What?"

"Sometimes the cocoons can be cooked and eaten like french fries!"

Zora shuddered. "You're making that up to gross me out."

"I'm not," Skylar said, laughing. "Here, try these on." Skylar handed her a couple of other dresses. At least they weren't too frilly or princess-y.

While she went along with her sister, Zora took the chance to retreat into her mind and analyze what she would do for the rest of the time they had to share the house with another family. She didn't want to offend anyone or come across as entitled or mean, but how she wished the adults had asked for the kids' opinion before committing to this disaster! This was the first time in history that two presidents' stays had overlapped, and judging by the past couple of weeks, the experiment wasn't exactly working. At least for her. It was nice to have Mom every evening instead of seeing her only on the weekends, though.

Still, Zora knew that Winnie and Ingrid were upset over their lost ferret, and the fact that they'd been tricked in their own house. Skylar wanted to think that the rift had been fixed, but Zora's instincts told her Winnie and Ingrid weren't done with their pranks.

She had history on her side to prove her point, and like the many generals and other military minds who'd lived under this hallowed roof, she'd find a way to play smarter than her rivals.

"That dress looks awesome on you! It makes you look so grown-up and tall!" Skylar said. She'd already gone through half her rack of clothes. "Annie," she called, "I think Zora's ready for you."

She opened the door before Zora could complain, and Annie, along with one of the stylists, a grandma type with sharp eyes, beckoned her over.

"Hi, Zora, sweetheart," the stylist said. "I'm Charlotte. Remember me?"

Zora was about to shake her head no, but Charlotte continued, "I'll be your fairy godmother. Turn around so I can tuck this in, baby. A zipper will make this dress more user-friendly, instead of all the buttons."

Skylar apparently hadn't fallen in love with any of her dresses. She'd left their makeshift dressing room to pore over a catalog with Annie and whispered excitedly about a new designer. Zora turned around and around in the dress, trying not to get poked by all the pins along the line where a zipper would go later. Suddenly she heard the voice of the head social secretary himself, Matthew Morton. Surprised, she jerked involuntarily and got stuck on her arm.

"Ouch," she said, rubbing her arm and getting poked in

the back. This dress was too tight!

"I'm so sorry," Charlotte said.

"It's okay," Zora said, trying to overhear what was going on in the office next door.

Zora's dad was talking to Matt. As the social secretary, he was in charge of organizing *all* the social events that happened in the White House. This time of the year, especially, he was a busy man. He was incredibly efficient, though. Mom was seriously thinking of keeping him for her administration. There was no need to reinvent the wheel, she always said.

Maybe in the years to come, Skylar could apprentice under him and help plan Mom's events. Then Zora would be free to spend her days in the Library or studying the art in the house. In peace. Alone.

But she liked Matt too, and always enjoyed talking to him. She quickly changed back into her jeans and sweater and headed next door.

Matt was already deep in conversation with Skylar and Annie. He was a tall, slender man in his thirties, dressed in a dark gray suit and a bright pink tie that complemented his dark brown skin.

Zora stood next to her sister, and Matt smiled at her.

"I've been waiting for the perfect moment to deliver these personally, but as you may have learned already, there's never a perfect moment at the White House."

"They're all perfect," Skylar added, beaming when Matt handed each of them an invitation on heavy stock paper with fancy golden handwriting.

Welcome to the White House celebration for Zora and Skylar! Come to the Green Room at seven, and meet America's most famous and beloved twins.
Hosted by Winnie and Ingrid

A party? Zora almost groaned but caught herself just in time. How could she ever say no to a personal invitation for a party in her honor?

"Who will be there?" she asked.

Matt smiled and looked at her dad, as if they'd been talking about her and expected this reaction. But really, was she being extra? Zora wasn't keen to go to an event where she might find googly eyes in a cup.

"The guests are the children of White House employees, dignitaries, and kids from Ingrid and Winnie's school," Matt said. "It will be a great way to meet people."

"Zora," Skylar whispered, elbowing her softly. "Javi will be there. For the article!"

Everyone waited for Zora's reply.

Noticing all the eyes on her, she motioned for Skylar to meet her by their dad's desk. Everyone could still see them, but at least they wouldn't be able to hear the whole conversation.

"I don't want to go!" Zora whispered. "We can't escape the official Christmas celebration or inaugural ball, but this? We don't have to go, Sky."

"What do you mean we don't have to? We're the guests of honor."

Zora huffed. "They could've at least asked if we were okay with it, don't you think?"

"Zora, they're trying! Besides, remember how much fun we had when we went bowling with them?"

As if she could see that Zora's stubbornness was cracking, Skylar handed Zora the invitation and a pen she grabbed from the desk. There were two little boxes to checkmark, *yes* or *no*. "We can't *not* accept their invitation. Imagine what it will look like if the magazines and tabloids get wind of the rumor! Besides, they already have the advantage of having known Javi the longest. We can't let them look like the best pair of first daughters."

It was time for them to show a unified front to the whole world.

"You're right," Zora finally said, and marked the box for *yes*.

SKYLAR

If this was a dream, Skylar never wanted to wake up.

If, five years ago, someone had told her that one day she and Zora would be the guests of honor at a party in the Green Room of the White House, she would have thought the person was lying to her. Or worse, mocking her. But here she was. She brushed her fingers over the silk wallpaper Jackie Kennedy herself had commissioned.

"It's really green, isn't it?" a girl asked. She had long, light brown hair, and a smattering of freckles covered her nose. The pink blush on her cheeks and the wide smile made her look very friendly.

"Yep," Skylar said. "When I saw it the first time, I was

shocked the rooms really are named after the color of their wallpaper."

The DJ played "YMCA," and Ingrid led a group of tweens in the dance.

"I'm Margarita," the girl said.

"And I'm Skylar Williams," she replied. "How do you know Winnie and Ingrid?"

Margarita shrugged. "I really don't. My father's the new Argentine ambassador. This is my first party at the White House."

"Mine too!" Skylar exclaimed. "I like your dress, by the way."

"And I like your headband," Margarita said with a smile. After a couple of seconds of silence, she asked, "What school are you going to?"

"Freedom Academy."

"Me too!" Margarita said, positively beaming, and then she sighed. "In Argentina I just ended seventh grade, but here they're having me do the second half again. To catch up on my English."

"Your English is really good!" said Skylar, realizing that Margarita's English sounded a little British and wondering how that had happened. "But at least we'll be together, and this way you'll have a friend already. Two friends, actually! My sister, Zora, will be in our grade too."

They spent the next few minutes talking about how different the school system was in Argentina, and how sad it was that Margarita was missing a whole summer of her life. The seasons are the opposite in the Southern hemisphere. She was supposed to be on summer vacation until March.

"But like you said, at least I already have friends."

"Let me call Zora over. You'll love her."

Skylar searched for Zora among the kids dancing.

She saw her next to Ingrid, who was apparently introducing her to a line of kids waiting to meet one of the Williams sisters. The tension of Skylar's shoulders eased when she saw Zora having fun.

Javi Rojas joined Zora and Ingrid, and soon they were all laughing. Ingrid took a little notebook from her dress pocket and wrote something in it.

"Come on, Margarita," she said. "Let's go join them."

They walked over and saw that Ingrid was now in her entertainer mode.

A hand on the side of her head as if she had an earpiece, she said, "All clear. Troublemakers One, Two, Three, and Four are asleep. Time to party."

"That's Agent Sisco," Skylar said to Margarita while everyone who knew Sisco laughed. Even the pitch of the voice was perfect.

When the laughter died down, Skylar said, "Everyone,

this is Margarita. She just arrived in Washington."

Margarita went around and kissed everyone on the cheek. "This is how we say hello in my country."

After introducing herself, Ingrid paused to write something down in her book.

"What are you writing?" Skylar asked.

"Ideas for her jokes," said Winnie, who Skylar hadn't noticed was in the group too.

"Jokes for what?" Skylar asked. Then she narrowed her eyes, but she still smiled. "Pranking innocent people?"

"For future performances," Zora said. "Remember she wants to be a comedian? Well, comedians have to practice and perfect their jokes."

Winnie rolled her eyes, but she did it good-naturedly. "It's her joke book. Her Book of Risas, as she calls it."

"Oh!" Skylar exclaimed. "I have a dream diary where I write my dreams and analyze them later."

"I have a notebook for words that have completely different meanings in American and British English, which is what I learned at school," said Margarita.

"My dad has a notebook with questions for press conferences, and another one for speculations and rumors," Javi added, bouncing with the beat of the music.

Winnie pressed her lips as if she was trying to suppress a smile and said, "Talking about rumors . . . tell me, what are you writing about the four of us?"

Javi made a mischievous expression. "That all depends, Ms. Win."

"On what?" Zora asked. "I hope you're not still upset that I threw the drink at your face during dinner. I'll always be sorry about that."

Javi, with the help of Ingrid, went on to rehash the events during that first dinner, and Skylar laughed until her stomach hurt.

Zora was blushing, but she still laughed.

"But that's the only hint of trouble in paradise anyone could even point at, and it wasn't really that bad," Javi said. "My contacts inside the house tell me you're all getting along super well. Bowling, cleaning together, now this party."

Winnie draped an arm around Skylar's shoulders and said, "Of course we're getting along! We, like, really we love you guys. You know that, right?"

Skylar met her eyes. "Of course."

She caught a glimpse of Agent Sisco standing at the entrance of the Green Room, a serene expression on his face, apparently relieved that the first daughters—present and future—were getting along. Agent Lee was moving her head to the sound of the music.

This was as good a time as any to apologize for the plastic-wrap fiasco. Skylar leaned closer to Winnie and said, "Sorry that the vase broke. That was an unintended consequence of our joke."

A blush spread all over Winnie's gorgeous face. Her eyes widened in surprise. "Thanks for apologizing," she said.

She had the best skin Skylar had ever seen in a teenager. Winnie was the picture of the perfect president's daughter.

Winnie shrugged. "I've said it already, but I am sorry that you got scared by the ice cubes that night."

"At least we can laugh about it now," Skylar added.

The kids playing Let's Dance on a giant screen were doing a perfect re-creation of one of the most popular viral dances. Ingrid had dragged Zora to the front line.

In that moment, two young men in dark suits and snow-white shirts, aides most likely, entered the Green Room carrying a large blue cooler, which was completely out of place on a cold December evening and in this elegant room.

"What's that?" Skylar asked Winnie, pointing at it.

Winnie was transfixed as two little girls with pigtails ran to the cooler and grabbed something from it.

"Popsicles!" one exclaimed.

The other kids left the dancing and the air hockey and ran to get a Popsicle too.

The music still blared from a portable speaker, but Skylar heard one of the little girls ask, "What flavor are these?" The surprised tone of her voice made Skylar's hair rise in alarm. The little girl handed the Popsicle to Javi Rojas, who looked at it and threw it back in the cooler with an expression of horror on his face.

Skylar's eyes widened as she covered her mouth with a hand. Something inside her screamed that she'd better find out what was in that cooler.

What if the poor ferret had been trapped in there? What if it was more googly eyes to prank everyone in the room, and then what if Javi thought that Skylar and Zora had been in on the collective joke and hated them forever?

She shoved the kids out of the way.

"Wait your turn!" one of little girls said, trying to push Skylar aside.

Skylar planted herself firmly in front of the cooler and looked in.

When she saw the contents, her exclamation of surprise wasn't princess-y at all. In fact, when she heard her own voice, she just felt distant shock at the idea that someone was screaming so unceremoniously, at the White House, at a party at which she was supposed to be the guest of honor, no less!

Feeling like she was having an out-of-body experience, she grabbed one of the Popsicles and took a long look at it. Inside each block of ice was a rolled-up piece of the underwear her sister had been searching for. The missing box of clothes!

She looked for her sister amid the sea of shocked faces.

Zora had been by the game console but was now standing right next to her.

There are so many myths about twins, like speaking in a made-up language (which Zora and Skylar had never done), or experiencing the same pain as your hurt twin who was miles away (which had never happened either, mainly because they were never far from each other), or accidentally dressing the same (which was impossible since their styles were so different).

This time, though, Zora and Skylar were synchronized in a way that would have earned them an Olympic gold medal if there was such an event as Escaping from a Room in the White House. As if they had suffered humiliation by panties before and knew exactly what to do, they each grabbed a handle of the cooler and ran out of the Green Room, straight toward the stairs to the third floor.

"How could they?" asked Skylar, panting with the shock of being betrayed.

"Hurry," Zora urged her, out of breath.

They ran past the young aides waiting outside the door, the maids, attendants, Secret Service people. No one stopped them as they dashed upstairs.

With another swift move, Zora opened the door to her room. Once they had deposited the cooler on the ground, they rummaged through its contents.

"Period underwear?" Skylar asked, holding one of the frozen pairs.

Zora turned red like a beet. For a couple of seconds, they looked at each other . . . and then burst into hysterical laughter.

Skylar laughed until her stomach hurt.

"You laugh, but it's my underwear they used!" Zora said, clutching her stomach.

"It's not like it had your name on it! But Javi Rojas, of all people, saw what it was and then saw us running out like we were firefighters on the way to a blaze. He'll put two and two together."

Maybe if instead of fleeing, they had had the coolheadedness to turn the joke around and make it seem like it wasn't their underwear, but Winnie and Ingrid's . . .

"I'm sorry I convinced you to go to the party," Skylar said.

Zora rolled her eyes. "It's not like it's your fault, Sky."

But Skylar still felt responsible.

"We'll have our revenge," she said. "As soon as the underwear thaws out, we will plan something. We're going to shake this house up."

WINNIE

Winnie's many mischiefs were starting to take their toll on her, but she'd doubled over with laughter when she saw the Williams girls running to the residence with the cooler.

But when Javi came up to her and shook his head, she felt a rush of shame that made her dizzy.

"That was really mean, Win. Why did you do it?" he asked.

She bit her lip. He didn't understand. Laffy was still lost because of the Williams girls, and they hadn't even offered to help look for him. "Listen, Javi. It was a joke. No one saw—"

"I did," he said, tucking his pen behind his ear. "I even held one. Didn't you see?"

Winnie lifted her chin defiantly. "The twins will get over it and we'll laugh about it later," she said. They had laughed after the incident of the horn. How was this different?

Javi shrugged and walked away before she could explain to him that she and Ingrid hadn't tried to humiliate anyone.

She went looking for Anjali, her friend, but she couldn't find her anywhere. Had she left already?

When she turned to ask Ingrid if she'd seen her friends from school, Margarita, the Argentine ambassador's daughter, walked up to Winnnie and asked, "Do you think Skylar will come back to the party? We were getting along really well."

Winnie shrugged. "I don't think so. Sorry."

"That's too bad." Margarita sighed. "I hope she's okay. I guess I'll see her at school."

Margarita fluttered at the fringes of a group of kids. Winnie hoped she hadn't ruined this newborn friendship between Skylar and Margarita, like her friendship with Anjali would be ruined if she didn't spend more time outside school with her.

Without the guests of honor, the party had lost its shine. Winnie was heading to her room when she came across two of the maids peering under a china cabinet.

"What's going on?" she asked.

One of them looked over her shoulder and said, "Your ferret is hiding underneath this cabinet, and I'm afraid he'll go into the vent."

Winnie lay on her stomach to peek under the piece of furniture, but it was too dark to see. "Laffy!" she called.

Either Laffy wasn't there or he was too scared to come out.

"Can we get Sisco to move this?" she asked, climbing back to her feet and trying to push the heavy wooden cabinet. It wouldn't budge.

The other maid replied, "Poor Sisco went to get some carpet cleaner."

"Carpet cleaner?" Winnie asked. She noticed Javi was watching, obviously eavesdropping and taking mental notes on everything that was happening.

"Carpet cleaner for the antique Persian rug," she said, pointing at a white blob in the middle of the expensive carpet. "Laffy ran across Sisco's feet and startled him so badly, Sisco dropped a cupcake—icing down, of course."

The other maid turned to Winnie and said, "We need to find that ferret before he destroys a historic artifact or something."

"How are we going to get him?" Winnie asked, feeling desperate.

One of the ushers who'd apparently been listening to the conversation stepped up to her side and suggested, "Maybe we can bring the cage from the third floor in case Laffy gets tired of running around."

"Or if he gets hungry for his treats," one of the maids added.

But Winnie doubted the plan would work.

"Laffy has never been in the wild on his own," she said. "If he finds a way out, then he's gone."

That night Winnie could hardly sleep, anxious for the morning to arrive. The next day, just a week from Christmas, she followed a trail of rumors around the house that she hoped would lead to Laffy, but every time, she ended up in the same place—in front of the third-floor Linen Room, where they'd moved the cage.

But each time, it was empty.

Just in case, she peeked into the laundry room to check if maybe Laffy had been locked in there, attracted by the warmth and the comforting scent of fabric softener.

"Laffy!" she called.

All she did was startle Lucinda, the main laundress, who'd been ironing linens with the peaceful hum of a dryer going round and round for company.

"Last I heard," Lucinda said, with a hand over her chest as if she was trying to quiet her galloping heart, "he was seen in the Green Room trying to get a cupcake. He shouldn't be able to come all the way up here, but I'm sure someone will get him. After all, he is priority number one for every department."

"He is?" Winnie asked, both relieved that she wasn't the only one looking for him and mortified for putting so many people out of their way to catch Laffy.

Lucinda nodded. "I heard that if he doesn't turn up by tomorrow morning, a ferret specialist is going to come for a consultation."

The more people involved in catching the ferret, the more chances for this disaster to leak to the press. Javi would keep the secret for the sake of their friendship, but not the rest of the media. Besides thinking she was a bad friend and host, he'd also think she was a bad pet owner. She usually didn't think about what people thought of her, but this was different. Javi was writing about her and her sister, and she didn't want one of the last stories about the López girls in the White House to paint her family in the worst light.

The Christmas ball was coming up soon and she wanted to find Laffy before then.

"I think someone said on the walkie-talkie that he could be in the subbasement," Lucinda added, before going back to ironing tablecloths.

"Ay, I better go see if I can find him there," Winnie said. "Thank you, Lucinda."

She took the stairs by the Linen Room to see if she would come face-to-face with the Williams twins. She wanted to make sure they hadn't taken the joke personally, that they understood that she and her sister were still joking around.

The Williams girls hadn't told anyone about the underwear prank, and Winnie knew that this time their revenge would be greater than a horn behind a door. Before she worried about what they were planning, though, she had to find her ferret.

In the subbasement, there were plenty of places where a small animal could hide. The cleanliness of the White House was incomparable, but it was still a big, old place.

"Laffy," she called softly, in case there was another worker nearby. She didn't want to startle anyone else.

There were rumors that ghosts, like Lincoln's, haunted the White House, but Winnie had never been scared of them. She felt sorry for them; they couldn't leave this house even after death.

She listened intently, but the only noises were the hum of the generators and compressors that kept the White House alive and running.

She was about to give up when a soft dooking sound told her Laffy might be nearby, excited to see her and go back to the safety of his cage. Her heart raced; he was so close!

Since he was easy to spook, she sat quietly behind an AC compressor. The quiet gave her a chance to breathe. If he sensed she was frantic, he'd never venture out of his hiding place, wherever that was.

"What are you doing?" a soft voice asked behind her, and Winnie jumped, screaming.

So much for not being scared!

The sound of tiny feet scurrying away told her Laffy had run to his next hiding spot.

She turned around and huffed. "Ingrid, what are *you* doing? I almost had Laffy, and now who knows where he's heading? If I don't find him soon, they're going to bring in a ferret specialist. And what if he chews through a historic artifact before they find him? Papi will make me pay for it. My allowance is still not that much."

"You can borrow some of mine," Ingrid said.

Winnie sighed. "You know what would be worse than having to pay for that?"

"What?"

"Laffy running out of the house to the gardens." Winnie shivered. Her greatest fear was the worst-case scenario of her beloved pet lost in the streets beyond the White House grounds, huddling under a bush in the rain. . . .

"We'll find him. You'll see," Ingrid said, patting Winnie's shoulder.

"How did you know I was here?" she asked, checking

behind a basket in case Laffy was hiding there.

Ingrid joined her in looking behind boxes and another compressor, although she had to know Laffy wasn't here anymore. "I heard you calling him."

"You heard me? How?" Winnie wasn't a history buff like Zora, but there had to be ways to make sure the conversations in the White House remained private. It was also true that the house was super old, and like any old house, it had both secrets and ways to reveal them to those who knew what to look for.

"I was already here in the basement," Ingrid said, and obviously guessing the following question in Winnie's head, she said, "Zora told me you'd come down here."

"Zora?"

"I saw her in the kitchen," she said. "She'd overheard Lucinda telling you someone had seen Laffy in the sub-basement."

"And why would Zora help you in any way?"

Ingrid shrugged. "I guess she feels bad for Laffy."

Winnie grimaced as if she'd tasted something sour. "What does she care? Isn't she upset at us? After all, the box we took had her name. . . ."

Now it was Ingrid's turn to shiver. "Don't even say something like that! We promised Mami that we'd be the best hosts. I told you they'd never forgive us for the underwear thing."

"We're not going to be outpranked by them. Now they have to drop it because they can't possibly top the Popsicles. I thought they'd go to their parents about it, which would have been bad, but now . . . What can they do?" Winnie said, going through the cabinets of the storage room across from the AC room, just in case Laffy had found a secret entrance.

Her main concern now was her ferret. She couldn't imagine leaving the White House without him.

Papi was busier than ever, but he made an effort to have dinner with just the family every chance he got. But tonight Mr. and Mrs. Williams had a commitment, and had asked if Skylar and Zora could share dinner with the Lópezes.

Sometimes during their meals, Papi would share things from work that concerned the whole country, and even the world and beyond when you considered space missions and stuff. He also asked about their days, and Winnie made sure she always shared something interesting with him—usually *American Ninja Warrior*, their favorite show—and Ingrid shared a joke.

But tonight, with Skylar and Zora at the table, the dynamic was different.

As always, Ingrid took it upon herself to fill the silence with information. Papi and Mami nodded and reacted at the right cues, but there was something going on that Winnie couldn't explain—and apparently Skylar and Zora felt the tension too.

Winnie wondered if it was her fault. And the more she worried, the worse her stomach hurt. She couldn't even take a bite of her chocolate lava cake.

Laffy was still lost, and Winnie felt worse about the incident with the frozen underwear. She never should've gone with it, but when she'd found the box in the storage room, she hadn't been able to resist the temptation. She'd found the idea on the same website that listed pranks. It had sounded so fun, but she hadn't really thought things through. Now her friendship with the Williams girls was definitely fractured.

Until something Zora said made Winnie come back to the conversation at the table as if she'd fallen off a cliff.

"Yes, but we'll still have security and Secret Service," Papi said.

Ingrid's face lit up as if he'd confirmed the existence of Papá Noel, the Three Kings, and El Ratón Pérez combined.

Winnie was confused. "Wait, what? What did you ask, Zora?"

Ingrid jumped in. "*I* asked if once we're in California we'll be able to go to summer camps, sleepovers, or around the neighborhood on our own, and Zora asked what about a security detail."

"Security detail?" Winnie asked.

Mami placed a calming hand over hers, explaining, "Even if we don't live at the White House and Papi isn't the president anymore, it still won't be safe for the family to be out and about like—"

"Like normal people?" Winnie snapped.

She regretted her outburst immediately when her parents looked at each other with concern, but it was too late to call the words back.

"At least you're used to having extra people around," Skylar said, like it was a good thing.

Having extra people around was exactly what Winnie absolutely didn't want. Especially not fake-smiling princess-looking girls who'd start planning what to do with your room before you even had time to move out. But her family didn't deserve her attitude, and Winnie felt bad for taking out her frustrations on them.

"It's all for our own good," Papi continued in a soft voice he reserved only for the family. "We'll get to open windows and stuff, at least . . . ," he said, with a tiny smile that made Winnie feel even worse for having a rotten attitude.

Her dad's service to the country had been invaluable. The years in the White House in the highest office of the land had meant so much for so many people, and missing a sleepover was nothing compared to all the lives his service had touched . . . but it still hurt that she would never have a normal life—and not because of anything she'd ever done.

"At least since the windows can't be opened and everything that comes in or out of the door is supervised, we know a certain animal isn't outside," Ingrid said quietly.

Winnie kicked Ingrid under the table. Papi hadn't missed anything, though. He narrowed his eyes at Winnie, and she shook her head almost imperceptibly.

Ingrid cleared her throat in a way that made it obvious she was changing the subject, and said, "We can still have a couple of wonderful parties while we're here."

Mami's face lit up, and Papi sighed as if the words had evaporated inside him when he saw her expression.

"The Christmas ball!" she said. "Are you girls excited?"

Zora grimaced, but Ingrid and Skylar replied in unison, "Yes!"

Skylar and Mami started talking about designer gowns, and Papi, Ingrid, and Zora talked about the music the band would be playing. Winnie felt so left out.

Until the light above the table flickered and eveything went dark. The emergency lights along the ceiling cast the dining room in an eerie red glow.

Skylar and Zora grabbed each other's hands, and Ingrid clung to Mami.

"What's going on?" Mami asked.

"Mr. President," Alice Sung said in a soft voice, quietly stepping into the dining room with a flashlight. "I'm sorry to whisk you away ahead of schedule, but there's been an incident with the power generator in the basement, so you won't be able to make your call from here. There is power in your office in the executive building. I'll have the New Zealand prime minister on the line with you on time, but it's a few minutes' walk there."

In the semidarkness, the four girls exchanged a look as if each pair of sisters was accusing the other of causing the electrical malfunction.

The electricity flickered again.

In her heart, Winnie had a hunch this had something to do with Laffy.

Papi took another bite of his flan, wiped his mouth with a napkin, and said, "Thanks, Alice. Lead the way. See you all later, princesas." He kissed Mami briefly and followed Alice out of the room.

Then Agent Sisco arrived and said, "Mrs. López, there's a security concern regarding the ball tomorrow. May I have a word?"

Mami rose from her chair. "Skylar and Zora, I'll walk you to your rooms, and then I'll join you, Agent Sisco. I hope the power returns soon."

"There is power on the third floor," Sisco said.

"Thank goodness." Mami sighed, relieved. "I'll still walk

you up, girls, but please let me know if you need anything while your parents are gone." Then she looked at Winnie and Ingrid and said, "I'll come over to say goodnight later."

She followed Agent Sisco.

Winnie fell a weight press on her shoulders.

She had to find Laffy before he created worse problems for everyone, destroyed a national heirloom, or got lost forever.

The next morning, the power had been restored all over the building, but Winnie couldn't get away to find Laffy. Her schedule was packed to the minute with photo ops, special performances at the house, and trying on the outfits for the ball.

But in the afternoon, Ingrid burst into Winnie's room and said, "Follow me! Kate told me Zora told her about an entrance to the subbasement where they found chewed pieces of electrical cord."

"And how did Zora know that?"

"She overheard the ferret specialist talking with Alice about it. They think Laffy was there!"

"We have to find him first, Ingrid," Winnie exclaimed.

The White House was in upheaval getting ready to receive the Christmas guests. Taking advantage of the fact that no one was paying attention to them, Winnie and Ingrid were soon running along one of the corridors underneath the subbasement.

"Aha!" Ingrid exclaimed in front of door 003.

"I've never seen this before," said Winnie, pushing it open with her hip. Ahead, the air smelled musty, and the room led to a tunnel. She walked ahead.

Ingrid pulled her back. "We need to get ready for the ball!"

"We're showered already," Winnie said, turning back toward the tunnel. "All we need to do is put on the dresses, and voilà!" Even to her ears it sounded as if she was trying to convince herself more than her sister that this was a good decision, but she didn't care.

The more they walked, the more they found new passages, like a labyrinth underneath the house.

"Are you keeping track of the turns?" Ingrid asked.

Winnie couldn't see her sister's face because the passageway was dark and their phone flashlight beams didn't reach more than a few feet ahead, but Ingrid's voice was worried. They should've been getting ready for the ball, not playing at being adventurers in the belly of the White House.

"Just follow me," Winnie replied, but she too was worried that she had no idea where they were going.

They continued quietly, although clanking and echoes

startled them every few seconds.

"How did we not know these passages were here?" Ingrid asked in awe.

"We were too little and too obedient to go exploring," Winnie replied, and although she hadn't intended it as a joke, Ingrid still laughed.

"I wish I could write that down so I won't forget it, Win," Ingrid said.

Winnie was glad her sister couldn't see her roll her eyes. Typical Ingrid. Only she would think of writing down a joke when they were walking in the dark heading to the Potomac for all they knew.

"If we'd known," Ingrid continued, "we could've mapped them out and created a ginormous escape-game thing with our friends."

Now it was Winnie who laughed. As if their parents would've ever let them do such a thing! If their parents ever found out they were in these tunnels, then Winnie could kiss her floor-to-ceiling windows goodbye.

Suddenly a rumbling sound tickled the soles of Winnie's feet. Ingrid dropped her phone and yelled, "What's that? A ghost?"

"Shhh," Winnie said, trying to muffle her laughter. "Someone's going to hear us. If anyone finds out we're down here, we're toast forever, Ingrid!"

They stood still, trying to make sense of the sound they were hearing.

"It's not a ghost. It's music!" Ingrid exclaimed. "The band is here!"

"Yikes! We need to get ready!"

"Let's hurry then," Ingrid said.

They ran hand in hand until they came across a fork in the tunnel ahead of them. Winnie thought of the movie *Labyrinth* and shivered, imagining goblins or other monsters hiding in the dark. In one of the tunnels, there was a giant pipe, the kind that carried heated or cooled air. It would also carry sound.

They stood right next to it, and Winnie put her hand over the hole. A warm blast hit her skin, along with an echo of the music—Luis Miguel singing the Spanish version of "Let It Snow."

There was a rustle like something big being dragged on the floor, and Ingrid and Winnie looked at each other, their eyes big like plates. But neither one could guess what it could be.

Winnie felt the minutes were ticking away. She didn't even have to glance at her phone to see they were supposed to be heading down to the ball with their parents.

"We need to turn back," she said. "We're never going to find him with all this noise."

Even in the feeble light of the phones, Winnie still saw how worried her sister looked.

Together, they made their way back, retracing their steps. But somehow they didn't end up in the AC room. Instead they came across an ancient wooden door with iron bars that let the frigid December air in.

"I hope Laffy didn't climb through these bars." Winnie shivered.

Once again, Ingrid was speechless.

José Feliciano's "Feliz Navidad" rang through every speaker and echoed outside in the garden. Winnie felt anything but happy. The house had secrets she had never even guessed, and she hadn't found Laffy, who could easily have escaped through this door.

INGRID

They tiptoed upstairs via a service staircase, dodging maids and valets rushing all over the place. The house was a whirlwind of activity, and no one looked at them twice.

As they finally arrived on the second floor, Winnie peeked down the hallway to see there was no one around to witness how late they were.

Ingrid sneezed, and Winnie sneezed right after her.

"We're horrible at stealth," Ingrid said, shaking her head.

"Let's not get sick." After a pause, Winnie added, "Although that's a good excuse for us not showing up."

Ingrid sent her a look.

"What?" Nagging suspicions were growing inside her,

but she didn't want to jump to conclusions. That was Winnie's specialty, after all.

"Nothing," said Winnie, sounding totally innocent, but not fooling Ingrid for a second.

Ingrid stopped walking, but Winnie continued as if she hadn't noticed. "I know you, Winnie Esperanza. And if you're thinking what I think you're thinking . . ."

Winnie laughed in that way of hers that made Ingrid suspicious of what her sister was about to say. "No, hear me out, Ingrid Belén. You. Me. In your room or mine, I don't care. Mami and Papi will have someone watch our door all night. We send for food. Watch a movie, eat pizza, wait out the night —"

Ingrid felt the pull of her sister's words. She didn't know how Winnie did it, but she was always getting her into trouble, and the worst thing about it was that Ingrid ended up following her willingly. Not anymore. She snapped out of Winnie's enchantment.

"Listen, it's our last Christmas ball at the White House!" she exclaimed, trying to keep her voice down. Music was coming out of the presidential suite, and their parents would be coming out ready for the ball any second. "We can't miss this! We just can't! I've been looking forward to it for ages. I went into the tunnels with you, and we found nothing. Now you come to the ball with me."

They'd arrived at the Closet Hall where their rooms

faced each other. And before they went their separate ways, they looked up at the same time. Winnie's reaction was the exact mirror of what Ingrid was feeling.

"What happened to us?" Winnie exclaimed. She was covered from head to toe in white dust.

Ingrid licked her lips. "Yuck! My lips taste like dust and paint. What if there are mice down there in those tunnels and we get a disease?"

"What if the paint has lead in it?" Winnie said.

Winnie definitely looked sick now. Ingrid had to make her feel better, or they would miss the ball for sure.

"Oh my gosh, Winnie. Look at your hair!" she said, laughing. "You look like Mamita Rosario."

Winnie pressed her lips to try to stop herself from laughing, but she couldn't. "Mamita Rosario? You look like Abuelito Ángel then."

They laughed about looking like their great-grandparents until they got tears. When Winnie wiped her eyes, she left a smudged trail on her cheek. She looked at her hand and sobered a little. "We definitely have to shower now."

"It's like that time we went four-wheeling in southern Utah, except with white dust instead of red," Ingrid said. "We can't put on our dresses for the ball over this grime. Mami will freak out if she sees us looking like old plaster statues."

Mami wouldn't think it was funny. Maybe one day they'd all laugh about this, but if their parents found out they'd gone on an adventure on such an important night, then no joke would ever make the situation right.

"Don't wash your hair," Winnie said, "It will take forever. Just shake off as much of the dust as you can."

"We can put dry shampoo on," Ingrid suggested. "It will be easier to put mine up in a bun that way. I'll look like Mami."

"Okay, but we have to hustle," Winnie said, gently pushing Ingrid toward her room. "Sorry, it was my idea to go looking for Laffy in those passageways."

A warm feeling came over Ingrid when her sister apologized.

"Let me know if you need help zipping up your dress," Ingrid said.

Winnie sent her a grateful smile. She winked at Ingrid and said, "Race you!"

"Race you!" Ingrid replied, adrenaline rushing through her.

Ingrid put on a shower cap, taking care not to wet her hair. If only they'd worn long sleeves, it would have been easier to rinse off all that dust. That one time after Zion National Park, she'd found red sand in her ears for weeks, no matter how well she cleaned them.

She scrubbed her skin hard, in record time so she'd be ready before Winnie.

But the room was drafty, and soon she was covered in goose bumps. She hurried to dry herself, but when she started getting dressed, she noticed that her skin looked green.

Was she seeing things? Had that image of a slightly sick-looking Winnie imprinted on her retinas so that now she saw the world through a photo filter? But something told her it wasn't her imagination.

When she didn't get enough sun in the winter months, her skin took on a greenish undertone. Mami joked about this all the time. When things got dire and they couldn't sneak in a trip to a sunny destination, Mami got a spray tan, which wasn't the same thing as pure vitamin D-soaked sunshine, but it helped in emergencies.

Ingrid had looked a perfect pale brown tone this morning when she'd showered after her swimming lesson. What had happened? Her heart started pounding when she saw two dark streaks on her legs.

She didn't know what was happening. Was she turning into an alien? Had she brushed against a poisonous substance in the underground tunnels?

She couldn't deal on her own, so she put on her fluffy robe and rushed across the hallway to Winnie's room.

The door was locked. Ingrid called her sister and knocked until her knuckles throbbed, but Winnie wasn't coming to the door.

Ingrid went back to her own room to get her phone, leaving her door open in case Winnie appeared.

Win!!! Open the door!

Ingrid felt time rushing by. She imagined a giant hourglass bleeding sand and dreams. The urgency of having to be ready was like barking hounds at her heels. If this was a movie, this would be super funny.

Now, though, she couldn't even remember a joke to make herself smile.

She looked toward the Closet Hall at the sound of rushing feet. It was one of the new maids in training, carrying a flower arrangement.

"Excuse me!" she said softly, trying not to startle the woman. "I got locked out of my sister's room. We were getting ready at the same time. Could you open the door for me, please?"

The woman's face lit up. "Of course, Ingrid!" She fumbled in her pocket and got one of the housekeeping master keys that had access to every room except the president's.

With a click, the door swung open. Ingrid could hear Winnie ranting in her bathroom.

Ingrid turned to the woman. "Thank you so much! See you later!"

She closed the door behind her and headed to her sister's bathroom. She tried to stomp so she wouldn't startle Winnie.

"Winnie!" she called out. Judging by Winnie's frantic

muttering, she imagined Winnie too was struggling with the same green-skin malady she was. Was it something they ate?

"Hey," Winnie said, looking at her like she was confirming her worst suspicions.

When Ingrid saw Winnie's face, she said, "Oh."

Winnie looked way worse than Ingrid. Her face had streaks of green across the forehead and cheeks that were impossible to confuse for anything other than sabotage.

"It's green Jell-O powder," Winnie said in an I-told-you-so voice that struck its mark in Ingrid's heart. "Industrial strength or something."

"How do you know?"

For a reply, her sister stuck out her bright green tongue. It would have worked super well a couple of months ago for Halloween for their matching witch costumes, but not tonight, when they should be looking their best for the last White House Christmas ball of their lives.

The other day Papi had reminded them that in the future they might be invited back to the house. Winnie had rolled her eyes at the mere suggestion, but Ingrid had thought with longing of the possibility. If she and Winnie made a scene tonight, though, there was no way they'd ever be welcomed in the White House again.

Ingrid touched the tip of her tongue to her own arm and she shuddered. Yep. It was Jell-O.

The pressing question was how, since there was no doubt of *who'd* done it.

"How did they do it?" Ingrid asked. "The water? The showerheads?" She pictured green jets coming out of the shower, but then her face would have been streaked too.

Winnie marched to the towel holder and grabbed an unused towel. "Here," she said, opening it wide for Ingrid to see.

True enough, Ingrid saw the greenish sparkles of dry Jell-O.

Then she glanced at the towels on the floor and saw distinct green streaks where the Jell-O's color had been activated with water when Winnie dried herself off.

Tentatively, Ingrid looked at the inside of her robe and with horror saw that indeed, the robe too had the traces of the latest prank by the Williams sisters.

Winnie rubbed her arm furiously with a white towel, but the green wouldn't come out. In fact, she made it worse, because the inside of every single towel they had was covered in dry green powder.

"Maybe they mixed it with something else," Winnie said. "Like a dye of some kind. I can't even tell if it's still on my skin or not."

Ingrid knew exactly what Winnie meant, but when she took a look at her sister, she knew they weren't imagining things. "It's definitely still on your skin."

"Not a trick of the light?" Winnie asked, desperation in her voice.

Ingrid shook her head.

Winnie muttered under her breath and then exclaimed, "What I want to know is how they got inside our rooms, and when."

Ingrid had the answers. "When we were in the tunnels! Zora knew exactly when I'd gone down. Kate knew you were in the subbasement looking for Laffy because Zora was the one who told her. She helped to—"

"To get us out of the way!" Winnie said, as if she could see the Williams sisters plotting. "It's obvious they've been keeping track of our moves."

"And how they got in our rooms is easy to guess. We never lock the doors when we're not in, because we've never had to before. And if the doors were locked, they could just ask housekeeping to let them in with one excuse or another. By the way, that's how I got into your room just now, so you know," Ingrid said.

Winnie's eyebrows shot up in horror. "We're not safe anymore. Maybe we should tell Mami?"

"Of course not!" Ingrid snapped. Her mind was whirling with thoughts of Zora and Skylar breaking into the rooms . . . when someone knocked on the door, startling her and Winnie.

"Who is it?" they both asked in unison, trying to sound

unfazed by the fact that they looked like really bad mermaid cosplayers.

"It's Rhea," a young woman's voice said, with a trace of concern underneath the cheeriness.

"I don't know her," Winnie mouthed.

"I'm one of the new maids," Rhea said. "Do you need help?"

Had it been Alice, Ingrid wouldn't have hesitated to tell her everything that had happened, even if it meant admitting fault, getting grounded, having to make reparations of some kind. Alice wouldn't tell anyone else—that is, until the right time to tell Mami. She wouldn't spread any gossip.

But if anyone else—especially Javi—found out about this . . .

"Girls," Rhea said again, "do you need me to come in and help you do your hair or something? Your parents are about to head down to the ball."

There was a pause in her voice that drove home the high stakes of their predicament. Papi and Mami were ready.

Ingrid and Winnie would be in so much trouble if their mom discovered they were still undressed and looked like lizards. No. She couldn't let everyone down like this. And she couldn't throw the Williams sisters under the bus. After all, it was just a joke.

She wanted to stay friends with Skylar and Zora after

this. She wanted to keep a good relationship with everyone. The thought that her actions had the potential to make a lot of people miserable made Ingrid's stomach churn. She had to put a stop to that too. If she got sick, their problems would only get worse.

"I got this," she told Winnie, shaking as much green powder as she could out of a towel and lifting it to her head.

She ran to the door and opened it just a bit so she could talk to the girl. "Hey. What's up."

The maid opened her dark eyes wide when she saw Ingrid. "What happened to your face? And your hair isn't even done! Oh my gosh! Let me in and I'll help you."

Ingrid had expected this reaction, and she knew exactly what to say. "Actually, my hair is totally done. I just kept the towel around it so that it wouldn't get messed up. Winnie and I are finishing up putting a little makeup on."

The woman's cheeks were still flushed red from stress, but her eyes didn't have that panicky look anymore. "Really? Can I help with anything, though?"

Ingrid smiled reassuringly. "Please, just tell my parents we're right behind them. We'll meet them downstairs in like five minutes."

The maid nodded and marched down the hall.

WINNIE

Not even thirty minutes ago, Winnie had wanted nothing more than to stay in bed and watch a movie, eat popcorn, and hang out with her sister. Anything rather than putting on a show she just didn't have the strength for.

But Ingrid . . .

She looked devastated at the prospect of missing this ball. Green skin or no green skin, Winnie was going to be there for her sister and show those Williams girls who were the true first daughters in the White House.

Somehow she'd get back at those girls for making Ingrid so upset.

"It's okay, Ingridcita. We got this. Don't worry."

Frantically, Winnie put her dress on and then helped

Ingrid get into hers. Imitating one of Mami's iconic looks, they arranged their hair in elegant low buns at the napes of their necks. It was surprisingly easier than usual. Maybe all the dust was helping the hair stay in place. Winnie didn't know; she was just grateful something was going well, at least.

For this event, the stylists had recommended high-neck, sleeveless dresses that didn't reach the girls' knees. It was supposed to be *the look* of the holidays. Winnie's dress was black and had a delicate lace panel over her collarbones. Ingrid's was burgundy velvet.

Why hadn't Winnie picked the long-sleeved dark green organza one when she'd had the chance? If she had, then she could have explained the greenish tint as a reflection of the fabric and bad lighting.

Her arms had horrible green streaks she didn't know how to get rid of, so instead of scrubbing herself raw, she rummaged in her closet for something that would match their dresses. Miraculously, she found a black cardigan for herself, but best of all, a burgundy one from last year for her sister. It had been an extra for one of the campaign events that Alice had ordered and never returned. Amid the mess, she also found a box of practical jokes. In a flash, she remembered the López administration's tradition of giving out white elephant gifts for their guests during Christmas. These were usually funny trinkets like novelty teacups, socks with pictures of Laffy on them, or weird-flavored lip balms.

What if Winnie and Ingrid planted a white elephant gift especially for the Williams sisters to get back at them for their green skin?

She wasn't sure what she'd find in the box, but on a whim, she brought out into the room, where Ingrid was waiting.

First, they needed to figure out their outfits.

"Yes!" Winnie said as she carefully helped her sister put the burgundy cardigan on. "It's the perfect match for your dress!"

"What do we do with our legs?" Ingrid asked.

"Nylons!" Winnie said with a flash of inspiration. She grabbed two unopened pairs of nylons from her underwear drawer.

The advantage of being disorganized was that there were surprises all over her room, and it must have been the adrenaline that helped her remember the exact location of the things she needed, or else a guardian angel who'd taken pity on her. The black nylons were perfect, and Ingrid's neutral ones had a sheen that disguised the green streaks on her legs.

"This is like magic!" Ingrid said.

"Now let's put on some makeup to hide the green on our faces!" Winnie said. "Yours isn't that bad, but look at me! Don't you dry your face after a shower?"

Winnie spread the foundation—which had been unopened and waiting for a special occasion—on both their faces. Well, this was definitely a special occasion. Good thing she and Ingrid had the same skin tone.

"Now let's go!" Ingrid said.

But Winnie shook her head.

The box of practical jokes was calling to her. While her fury had smoldered to embers, she'd come up with a plan to get back at Skylar and Zora—during the ball, where they'd least expect it. They'd think she and Ingrid had given up.

Winnie was super competitive, though. After all, you couldn't spell Winnie without Win.

INGRID

There's always a moment just before the point of no return, when you can decide a plan is too risky or dangerous— that just imagining it was enough.

Many times in that short stretch of White House hallways between her room and the ball, Ingrid had the impulse to tell Winnie to forget all about her payback prank.

Being united against a common enemy had been fun enough, but if their new plan worked, then they'd have to face serious consequences.

The ushers and maids looked up and smiled when they saw Winnie and Ingrid running like Cinderella hurrying to make the ball.

The twins had gone too far when they decided to break into their bathrooms. And then to stain them with green Jello-O!

Ingrid was stunned by the Williams sisters' audacity.

But when she really looked at the scene in front of her, her outrage at the twins briefly disappeared.

Ingrid had attended many parties as a first daughter, but she was swept away by the wonder and grandeur of the Christmas ball. From the staff to the volunteers, everyone had outdone themselves in making the house look radiant. The guests in gorgeous dresses and tuxes chatted and danced among the glittering decorations, celebrities mixing with former staff and friends who had known the family forever.

She was sure going to miss this magical place!

"Ay ay ay!" Winnie said next to her, gazing at the sea of guests.

Ingrid reached out a hand to rub at a streak of green on Winnie's cheek. In this magnificent lighting, the color was a little more noticeable than it had been in her room.

"What's next?" Winnie asked, a mischievous glint in her eye.

"Plant the package," whispered Ingrid, worried someone would overhear her.

A hand fell on her shoulder, and Ingrid and Winnie both jumped.

Ingrid recovered first. "Alice!" she exclaimed. "You scared us!"

"Sorry," she said. "But where were you, girls? I've been looking for you everywhere. So has Javi. For some reason, Zora and Skylar were worried that you two wouldn't be joining us."

For the first time, words abandoned Ingrid. The twins sure had nerve! But she couldn't let Alice see how angry she was at the mere mention of Skylar and Zora.

"Speaking of twins, where are they?" Winnie asked.

Alice pointed toward a cluster of kids dancing by the DJ. "I just saw them there with Javi."

"Thanks," Winnie said. "I need to leave this present by the tree. BRB." She was gone in a blink, beelining toward the giant Christmas tree in the middle of the Blue Room.

Alice looked at Ingrid for an explanation. Ingrid fought the urge to reveal that inside that innocent-looking box tagged with the twins' names was a glittery revenge. She swallowed the knot in her throat, her heart hammering in her chest, in sync with the music as her sister dodged among the guests, the staff, Mami and Papi, and the Secret Service agents mingling in the crowd.

"You girls brought your own white elephant gift?" Alice asked, narrowing her eyes as if she were trying to read the tiny label from the other side of the room. "Is it for someone in particular?"

Ingrid shrugged and her face warmed. "Not really," she lied. "We just wanted to contribute to the . . . festivities."

Alice looked like she was about to say something when a tinny voice crackled in her earpiece. She put a hand over her ear and nodded. "I'll be right there." Then, turning back to Ingrid, she said, "Have fun and behave." She wove among the guests and headed out to the garden.

Ingrid exhaled in relief that Alice was gone. The secret prank was safe, and Winnie had reached the goal. The booby trap was one more innocent box amid the sea of presents for the guests who kept arriving.

Ingrid gave Winnie a thumbs-up.

"Ingrid!" Javi called, and she turned around to say hi to him.

But when Ingrid looked back for her sister, Winnie was nowhere to be seen. Ingrid didn't know what to do. She was afraid of leaving her post in case she missed the moment the glitter went off. She started heading toward the tree to guard the bomb when a man she'd never met before beat her to it and grabbed the present.

Her heart stopped in panic. "Excuse me," she said, but the man didn't hear her.

He was trying to read the label, and then he shook his head and passed it to a woman wearing a bright red dress. Ingrid followed her and reached her just in time as the woman handed the present to one of the ushers. She didn't know his name. He must have been called in for the ball. He took a look at the label and resolutely headed over to a woman in a black dress and an earpiece that marked her as part of the event planning department.

The woman looked at the label suspiciously and shrugged. She handed it back to the usher, who went looking around the crowd.

It seemed that he wanted to give the present to the twins. Where was Winnie?

She was going to miss the twins' reaction! Ingrid felt a rush of adrenaline as she frantically searched for her sister while trying not to lose sight of the present.

Beads of sweat sprang along her hairline as she ran all over the room, following the present passing from hand to hand.

For the first time, she understood the saying her mom used when she was particularly stressed: *My heart is in my throat!*

WINNIE

Winnie left the present under the tree, and when she lifted her gaze, she saw two beady black eyes looking at her from under a table.

"Laffy!"

The last place Winnie had expected to find her ferret was at the Christmas ball, but here he was.

Before she could call him to her, the ferret darted off and scurried between fancy high heels and shiny polished shoes. Perhaps he too had been lured by the delicious scent of so many of his favorite foods—tamales, empanadas, and sweet bread. She wished she could stop to sample them, but she had a mission.

She tried to keep a low profile and headed on over to the

vase behind which Laffy's pointy nose was now poking out.

Unfortunately, because she rarely made an official public appearance, everyone wanted a photo with her. No one mentioned her green skin, but she couldn't go one step without someone interfering with the mission to save her ferret.

"Of course. Of course," she said graciously. Cell phones were forbidden at most White House gatherings, but the cameras-to-humans ratio at this ball was just unreal.

She was about to make a run for it, and pretend she couldn't hear people calling her, when a beloved voice stopped her in her tracks.

"How about a picture with old Eugene, Winnie?" asked one of the retired ushers.

"Eugene!" she screamed, and jumped into his arms.

He'd worked at the White House for decades and had retired when Winnie was ten.

"So great to see you!" she said.

He introduced his mother and sister to Winnie, and she didn't even have to fake a smile for the photo. He'd always been so kind to her, especially during the first years when her parents were trying to find a rhythm in their new lives. Eugene had taught Winnie to read by helping her sound out the labels on the paintings and sculptures all over the house.

Eugene didn't comment on her green skin. He was always discreet and gentlemanly, but she hoped the reason he hadn't mentioned anything was because the makeup had really covered up the embarrassing green streaks. The whole time she was smiling at the camera, she was also conscious of the two Williams sisters looking down from the stair landing, pointing at something underneath one of the buffet tables. Winnie followed their concerned gaze and saw Laffy's tail twitching underneath the long tablecloth.

"I can't believe how much you've grown, Winnie-loo," Eugene said, with such emotion that Winnie couldn't help smiling.

She talked with Eugene for a couple of minutes, but she turned toward the table every few seconds so she wouldn't lose sight of Laffy.

After a while, Eugene said, "Now go play with your sister and your friends. It was great to see you."

He sent her off, and Winnie tried to make an effort not to run. She'd seen Laffy's shadow weaving among the furniture.

She had to catch him before someone realized that a ferret was sniffing around the canapés.

If anyone thought Winnie hadn't been a responsible pet owner . . . she didn't even want to imagine the drama that news would cause.

For the sake of family, country, and honor, she had to catch Laffy.

She ran, dodging photographers, lamenting that she'd decided to wear her first pair of high heels tonight. Worst timing ever.

Just when she was about to intercept Laffy between two tables, she heard Papi's voice calling her name.

She whipped around to look over her shoulder, and she crashed into a mountain. It realistically took her less than a second to recover her smile, but her insides were rattled, her spine realigned, and her chakras unblocked by the collision.

She searched for the cause of her accident, only to look into Agent Sisco's icy blue eyes. For his next career, he could consider auditioning to be a basilisk. She was paralyzed by the force of his stare.

"The ferret. The tree" were his enigmatic words, but inside Winnie's mind, they connected.

Time slowed down. She turned toward the highest fir tree, the one decorated with ornaments sent by children from all over the world. Her parents had received them as presents during state visits and as gifts throughout the year. Winnie had helped Mami choose the best ones for the main tree in the Blue Room, the one they'd received at the beginning of the month. Right before the twins had moved in.

If Laffy made it to the tree, then she and Agent Sisco could kiss the chance of rescuing the ferret goodbye. They had to stop him before he took refuge in the sharp needles and priceless ornaments.

With a glance of understanding, they darted in opposite directions.

"Winnie! A few words!" Javi called out.

"In a minute, Javi!" she said in his general direction.

Since Sisco was wearing a dark tuxedo like the great majority of the men, she quickly lost sight of him.

Winnie speed-walked with only one goal in sight. Her breath came in short gasps.

Laffy, obviously overwhelmed by the sensory overload after spending a life of relative quiet and peace in his cage in Winnie's room, darted around people's shoes.

When she was only a few feet away from the giant tree, there was one of those miraculous pauses in the music and the chatter. A second of thundering silence reverberated in the room, and Winnie called gently, "Laffy!"

The ferret looked at her with terrified beady black eyes. Laffy was paralyzed, as if his whole life was flashing in front of him. Winnie wished she could just stop the party and ask for everyone's help. But she didn't want to embarrass her parents.

The music and the chatter resumed, and no one around her noticed that she was on a life-or-death quest. She ducked under a table, hoping the tablecloth would conceal her.

"Laffy!" Winnie called again.

At the sound of her voice, a waiter who was passing by with a tray full of goblets of eggnog got so startled that he also yelled. The tray went flying into the air.

Winnie saw in slow motion as the eggnog flew in all directions, golden ribbons of sugary holiday calamity barely missing actresses, models, and influencers, and worst of all, Senator Demetria King, who had faced President-Elect Williams in the primaries and lost. The goblets shattered in twinkling music. Winnie stared at the mess as she crawled out from under the table.

She'd tried her best not to create a scene, but now it was too late. She was so close to catching Laffy that she could almost feel his little fuzzy body in her hands.

"I'm so sorry!" Winnie exclaimed, but she kept running toward Laffy.

She wished she could stop to help the waiter, but in true White House fashion, an army of ushers, maids, and housekeepers was right on task, cleaning up the mess, gathering the glass, and reassuring guests who'd missed disaster by a fraction of a second.

Ahead of her, Sisco was closing in on Laffy, his arms outstretched just like hers.

They had the ferret.

Just one more inch . . .

"Rat!" a woman's voice wailed.

Sisco swerved to squelch that PR catastrophe, and Winnie kept running. From the corner of her eye, she saw the horrified woman backing up quickly, her hand clasping her neck as if she was afraid the supposed rat would turn into a vampire and come bite her. The woman bumped into one of the smaller fir trees that lined the walls and yelped.

The sound startled Laffy enough that he jumped, and in a motion that left Winnie breathless—it was a gymnastics feat—he grabbed onto one of the main tree's branches and pulled himself up to hide among the lights and needles.

Sisco and Winnie looked at each other in utter defeat as the Williamses watched in shock from the stair landing.

SKYLAR

If they had scripted the whole thing, it couldn't have turned out better.

Skylar's only regret was that she and Zora still didn't have their phones back. She'd have loved to sneak hers into the party to take video of the green-tinged López sisters running in all directions—Winnie trying to catch the poor ferret, and Ingrid chasing her sister.

Skylar almost felt bad for them. After all, the fact that Laffy the ferret was still lost was technically her fault. If it hadn't been for the horn strategically perched behind the bathroom door, poor Lafayette would still be living his best life in his cage. But at the same time, the López girls had brought this upon their own heads by making Zora cry.

"Maybe we should help them get the ferret," Zora suggested.

"No," Skylar said. "The poor little ferret will be all right. What we need now are photos to keep this amazing ball in our memories. I'm going to go talk to Javi. Wait a sec."

Zora nodded. "Part two of Operation Shaking Up the House?"

Skylar beamed at her.

They beelined in opposite directions, each with her own secret mission.

Skylar headed to Javi. This was her chance to make sure he featured them as the better pair of first daughters in his article for *Verified Teen*.

"Hey, Javi!" she said. "How's the research for your article going?"

He shrugged. "I'd like to get a picture of the four of you together. That's pretty much all I need before I send the final draft."

"I'm sure there are tons of pictures the official photographers can send you."

"There isn't even one! Every time the four of you are in the same room, something dramatic goes down, Zora," he said.

"I'm Skylar," Skylar corrected him, trying not to sound annoyed.

They'd met so many times before, but he still couldn't

tell her and Zora apart! She and her sister weren't even wearing the same kind of dress!

"You've known Winnie and Ingrid for a long time?" she asked.

"Since they first moved in," he said. "I started coming to briefings and press conferences since as soon as I was old enough to sit still."

"You sad they're moving out?"

Javi looked over the crowd as if he was searching for the López sisters. "Yes and no," he said. "I'm going to miss them, but living here in the spotlight isn't easy. . . . Winnie has been having a hard time lately. But I'm sure you know that. Besides, I hope we can keep in touch. At least to exchange some gossip."

"And why is this piece for *Verified Teen* so important to you?" Skylar asked.

Javi beamed one of his dazzling smiles. "I've always wanted to follow in my parents' footsteps. Both of them are reporters. I got this chance to prove myself, and I want to do the best job."

"I'm sure you'll do well," she said. "So you only need pictures to finish your assignment?"

Javi scratched his head. "Actually, yes. I need more photos of all of you girls."

"Didn't my sister send you a few already?"

"She did. But like I said, I'd love some shots of the four

of you together." He looked past Skylar and pointed. "The López girls are over there. Why not go and get some nice shots now? I have my camera in my backpack."

She didn't particularly want to spend time with the López girls, but she couldn't think of a way to get out of this predicament.

"Sure," she said, and followed him.

Ingrid and Winnie were talking in furious whispers, eyes darting to the big Christmas tree.

The music was too loud to overhear what they were arguing about, but judging by their expressions, neither one was happy.

Javi walked up to them, and when he looked at the tree, his eyes widened in shock. But he seemed to come up with an idea, because he pointed to Skylar as he said something to Winnie.

At the sight of Skylar, Winnie grimaced. She quickly tried to disguise it with a smile, but it was too late.

Ingrid placed a hand on her sister's shoulder. Funny how, at eleven, she was the youngest of them all, but she was also the tallest, and judging by the expression on her—greenish—face, the most unforgiving too. She didn't even pretend to smile at Skylar.

If it hadn't been too late to pull back the next section of Operation Shaking Up the House, Skylar would have called a truce, forgotten about the ferret ice cubes and the underwear, and put this all in the past.

But considering the clay-mask looks on Winnie and Ingrid, Skylar was sure they wouldn't forget about the plastic wrap or the green skin anytime soon.

Skylar looked up at the tree, and although she'd guessed what was up there, she still gasped at the sight of a pointy face peeking out through the needle-y branches. She placed a hand over her heart as if the gesture could steady its rhythm. "Oh my," she said, "Is that . . ."

"The ferret," Javi said.

Winnie pressed her lips together hard, and the force of her gaze made Skylar step back. Right into Javi.

"Sorry," Skylar said, mortified for having stepped on him.

"It's okay," Javi said, brushing the top of his shoe against the opposite calf, supporting himself on a little table full of dirty glasses and plates.

Ingrid and Winnie exchanged a cryptic look.

Skylar felt a knot grow in her throat and wished she could swallow it down.

She wanted to run away from here and lock herself in her room and never see these people again. Not her room in the White House, this gilded cage. *Her* room, in their old house.

The music was strident in Skylar's ears. She had the urge to cover them up with her hands, but she couldn't without seeming like she was failing at being a future first daughter. She felt like she was having an out-of-body experience, still keenly feeling Winnie's killer glances, the people dancing around them, the music's volume increasing by the second, and the pointy face of the poor ferret looking down at her from the tree, asking her what evil it had done for her to put him in this situation.

Her eyes prickled, and she blinked quickly to dispel the unwelcome tears. She wished she and Zora hadn't split up for this part of the plan.

"We just need to wait for him to climb down of his own free will," Javi was saying. "If we try to do something drastic, we could create an escándalo."

"I guess that while we wait, you can take some photos, Javi?" Ingrid asked. "I mean, what else are we going to do?"

"We might as well," he said, and took out a fancy camera from his backpack.

Winnie was still stubbornly facing the tree, but Ingrid turned back to look at Skylar. "Come closer, Skylar. Let's get some pictures."

She flipped that internal switch and quickly put on her entertainer persona. Maybe it was too late to fix her friendship with Ingrid and Winnie, but Javi would still be covering events at the White House for many years to come, and Skylar definitely didn't want to start on the wrong note.

"Come here and stand between us," Ingrid said with a wide smile that gave Skylar the chills.

"Yes," Winnie added in a sweet voice that sounded so wrong coming out of her mouth. She seemed nothing like the mischievous but really down-to-earth friend who hadn't hesitated to let Skylar borrow her bowling ball.

She had no choice but to stand in between her two frenemies and hope for the best.

"Turn to this side, Winnie," Javi said, his eyes squinting. "The lighting is horrible next to the tree. Maybe it's the twinkling lights?" He looked down at the lens and wiped it with a cloth.

"Oh," Winnie said in that eerie cheerful voice. "Do we look a little green?"

Skylar looked at her and smiled sheepishly. Winnie's eyes told her she'd pay for the prank.

Ingrid reached over behind Skylar's back, and a second later, Winnie said, "Ouch."

Had Ingrid pinched her? Skylar hoped Winnie didn't think it had been her! She didn't want to be in the middle of this argument between the López girls, but she couldn't escape.

Javi, oblivious to the silent war raging right in front of him, said, "Yes! Now that you mention it, you, Winnie, look a little greenish. But it's weird. It's like streaks. . . ."

He obviously didn't want to say anything insensitive,

but Skylar just knew Javi was thinking that only Winnie and Zora had that greenish tint. He was just too much of a gentleman to offend anyone.

Javi clicked a few photos and then looked over his shoulder. "If only Zora was here too! Then everything would be perfect!"

"I'll go get her!" Skylar said. "I know where she is!"

Before anyone could stop her, she slid out of the group. Zora would need time for the next part of their prank, and Skylar had volunteered to give her as much as needed. Since they wanted to avoid any kind of suspicion thrown their way, Skylar would pretend to be both Zora and herself during the last part of the ball.

She'd always wanted to swap identities at school, but Zora had always said no.

What was the point of being identical twins if not for this kind of situation?

Smiling in anticipation, she wove through the multitudes until she found an out-of-the-way cloakroom where there were individual changing stalls.

One of them had a sign that said OUT OF SERVICE in Zora's perfect handwriting. Just like they'd planned.

Skylar opened it and saw, with relief, her sister's dress. The backpack they'd left earlier with a different outfit for Zora was empty. Skylar quickly shed her dress and put on Zora's. After a couple of deep breaths, she headed back to the ball.

By the time she'd left the cloakroom, she'd channeled her sister. If anyone was an expert on Zora, it would be Skylar. She knew the way Zora angled her face to the side to better pay attention to things, the stern set of her jaw when she was studying someone or something. The way her voice was a little lower in pitch than Skylar's.

The excitement of doing something she'd only ever seen in movies replaced her fear with adrenaline.

She was practically floating on air when a hand fell softly on her shoulder. She turned around and saw it was Agent Lee.

Agent Lee was super sharp and observant. Mom only chose the best of the best to guard Skylar and her sister. This was the trial by fire. If Skylar passed . . .

Skylar was giddy about the possibility of tricking Lee, but she remembered that she was Zora now, so she composed her face in a serene but impatient expression. "Hey, Lee, have you seen my sister?"

Agent Lee motioned behind her and replied, "She was right there with the López girls." She turned and her eyes widened. "Oh, she was there less than a minute ago." She placed her hands on her hips and tapped her black shoe.

Agent Lee deserved better shoes than the ones that looked like Agent Sisco had chosen them without regard for beauty, only thinking of utility. Skylar made a mental note to suggest some cute loafers for the officers who wanted to wear something more chic.

"Why did you guys split up, Skylar?"

Skylar's heart skipped a beat, but at least her mind clicked right on cue. "I'm Zora," she said.

Agent Lee blushed to the tips of her ears. "I'm sorry to confess that I'm still having a hard time telling you apart. I thought the different dress colors and different hairstyles would help, but . . ."

Skylar smiled her Maleficent smile. Inwardly, so she wouldn't blow her cover.

"It's okay. It happens."

Agent Lee raked her fingers through her hair and asked, "Wasn't Skylar with you?"

"She was with the López girls and Javi. One of the ushers told me she wanted me to meet them here."

The agent narrowed her eyes. "And where were you?"

"I just needed some fresh air," Skylar said, trying to channel her inner Zora.

Agent Lee nodded. "Of course. Just try to stay in sight. There's too many people at this ball."

"Sure," she said, and headed toward the kids still guarding the tree.

"Where were you?" Winnie asked in that same voice that had chilled Skylar before. But now that Skylar was pretending to be Zora, she had to react differently. Her sister would be unfazed by the cold tone. She wouldn't have noticed there was something different with Winnie, so Skylar smiled and said, "I found this beautiful table with miniature White Houses in a tiny room next to the Secret Service office. I lost track of time."

It was exactly what Zora would've done. Javi's and Winnie's eyes glazed over with boredom. *Score!*

Ingrid smiled. "Aren't they the best? Which one was your favorite?"

Skylar was glad her sister had been giving her multiple tours, including lectures, every single day since they'd been here. She remembered the one thing that had called her attention.

"I loved the bicentennial Fabergé egg with the White House inside!"

She *had* liked it the best, but now she had to find the words her sister would use. So she said, "The details of the tiny Ionic columns! It's a piece of art. I spent hours analyzing them, and they're exactly like the real ones. You know, James Hoban's original design was modeled after the Leinster House in Dublin, Ireland, but it didn't include the north and south porticos."

There was a pause in which she delighted in the surprise on the faces of the kids. She hoped they wouldn't ask any more questions, because this was as much as she knew about the White House architecture. She shouldn't have worried, as Winnie, Ingrid, and Javi were completely speechless.

"Should we take a photo?" Skylar/Zora said.

"Yes!" said Javi.

Winnie and Ingrid exchanged a look.

"I'll stand in the middle with my two best friends," Skylar/Zora said before the López girls could add a word. She hooked her arms into the girls', and smiled Zora style—that is, with pressed lips.

After Javi had snapped a few pictures, Skylar/Zora said, "I guess I'll go look for Skylar. Did she say where she was going?"

Winnie rolled her eyes. "She went looking for you."

"I'm sure she's coming back soon," Ingrid added.

But Skylar was already heading out.

Her dress was still in the stall, which meant her sister hadn't yet returned from her secret mission. Skylar changed back and returned to the ball.

By now, Winnie was sipping a Shirley Temple near the table where waiters were bussing the dirty cups. She glanced up at the tree every few seconds. There was no sign of Ingrid or Javi.

"Hi," Skylar said, and Winnie got startled.

Skylar smiled brightly. So many minutes of not using her smile, and her face had missed the exercise. "I can't believe Laffy's up there. I wish I could climb that tree to get him."

"You wouldn't know how," Winnie said. "You're too much of a delicate princess."

Skylar relished that she was free to word spar with Winnie. "You say 'princess' as if it's a bad thing. You look more princessy than I do."

Winnie looked down at her dress and then raised a finger to suggest, "A lizard princess, you mean?"

After an awkward silence, Skylar asked, "Where's Javi? Is he all done taking the pictures he needs?"

Winnie shrugged one shoulder. "He's looking for you with my sister."

"I'll go find them, then," she said.

"Don't get lost, twin."

Fire rose inside Skylar. Why could Winnie be nice—charming, even—with Zora and not with her?

She went looking for Javi, who was taking photos of Ingrid by the staircase that led to the cloakroom. "Javi!" she called.

"Did you see your sister?" Javi asked.

Skylar forgot if there was anything she shouldn't know. On TV, twin identity swapping looked so easy, but it was exhausting! Maybe this was why Zora had refused to pull this kind of prank on people.

Skylar wanted a Shirley Temple too, but she couldn't risk staining her lips, or doing anything that could give her ruse away.

"No," she said. "Is she still not here?"

"You two keep missing each other!" Ingrid exclaimed. "I wanted to talk to her about the White House architecture. She knew so many things I'd never heard about before!"

Skylar nodded and said, "Well, it is a very big ball. People get lost easily."

At that moment, Agent Lee walked in her direction. "Have you seen your sister?"

Skylar whipped around and said, "I'll go find her."

"No!" Agent Lee said. "I don't want to lose you now. Stay with me."

Skylar had to stay put, wondering where her sister really was by now. She should've been back from the tunnels long ago.

"I'm going to the ladies' room," she said to Agent Lee, and before anyone could stop her, she dashed to the cloakroom and changed into Zora.

On her way back to Agent Lee, she passed her mom.

If she'd been dressed as herself and not surrounded by a million people at the White House, she would've fallen into her mom's arms and cried her eyes out about being exhausted. But being dressed as Zora, she obeyed her mom's silent beckoning and stood by her side while she talked to someone she recognized from TV.

When the man left, her mom turned to her and said, "Please stay with Agent Lee. She's worried about you. Where were you?"

Skylar hesitated and remembered to channel Zora just in time. "Looking at some paintings."

Mom smiled. "Now go back and hang out with the López girls. We need to quash the rumors of you four having a feud. I want at least a single photo of all of you together, please."

"Your wish is my command," Skylar said, in a perfect imitation of Zora's voice.

She walked to where Agent Lee was waiting for her and tried to channel her inner Zora again. Being so composed was way more work than she imagined. But she didn't really know any more interesting White House facts, and at moments like this, it was easier to stay quiet.

ZORA

Zora loved history. But more than anything, she loved the thrill that came from finding out obscure bits of history and the adventures that followed them.

She'd been studying the public White House floor plan for months and months when she was supposed to be doing math. One night on the campaign trail, way before her mom had even won the nomination, Zora had come across an interesting footnote in one of the maps she'd been poring over.

She dug for weeks, trying to discover if there was any truth behind the rumor that there were secret tunnels underneath the White House. She'd never been able to come to any conclusions, and the Secret Service agents hadn't wanted to reveal any of the great mansion's secrets to her before they knew for sure that Theresa Williams was going to win the presidency. Or maybe they just didn't know anything about it and didn't want to admit it.

But as soon as her family moved into the White House, Zora was studying the movement of people and the flow of the building, and she was convinced there had to be secret connections between rooms, even if the Lópezes had never found them.

At first Zora hadn't found anything concrete behind doors and the backs of closets. All she gained after her exploring was a headache and a scolding by Skylar that she was becoming obsessed with these secret passages.

The big breakthrough came to her when she was in the shower one rare lazy Sunday morning. She was thinking about how to rescue Winnie's poor ferret, an innocent casualty of the war between the first daughters, when her mind wandered to the history of pets in the White House and how in the past there had even been sheep on the lawns.

She didn't realize the connections her brain was making until she thought of a small door in the subbasement kitchen, the one where the staff gathered for meals.

There had been a little table blocking the door, and when Zora asked Agent Lee what was behind it, the agent had deflected her attention to something else. Zora had forgotten about it, but a part of her subconscious obviously hadn't.

That day, she'd set out on her own to discover if her idea was a fluke. She'd felt like Indiana Jones, Lara Croft, or that guy from the old National Treasure movies. Instead of complaining about how it wasn't fair that now her life had so many new rules, she'd decided to use the resources she had.

Her good attitude was rewarded when she found a tunnel from that tiny door to the Library. Zora believed she'd been dropped into the best adventure of her life.

After investigating the tunnels night after night, she'd found two passageways that led from the Library to Ingrid's and Winnie's rooms. They also connected the rooms behind the craft closet, which had been an amazing discovery, because now she and Skylar could sneak into each other's rooms without anyone tracking every single one of their movements.

She was also a little alarmed that the rooms could connect. This knowledge could be dangerous in the wrong hands, and she was only sharing it with her sister, the one person she trusted other than her parents. But their parents would freak out if they knew. Mom, with her strict rules about privacy and consent, would go blocking every secret tunnel, and Zora didn't want to give up the fun.

Earlier in the evening of the Christmas ball, she'd left her dress in the cloakroom and changed into a black outfit— really just leggings and a turtleneck left over from last

Halloween, when she'd been Jiji the cat to Skylar's adorable Kiki the witch—that would let her move with freedom and blend in with the shadows.

She wasn't scared of the dark, but she imagined a thousand tiny eyes looking at her. She said a little prayer that there wouldn't be anyone waiting to ambush her. She'd freaked out at that first prank, and she couldn't forgive Winnie and Ingrid for scaring her so badly. She'd teach them a lesson!

She had to stoop a little as she walked in the dark tunnel, trusting her memory. Finally she opened the door at the back of Ingrid's closet, and the motion sensor turned the light on, momentarily blinding Zora. She waited a couple of seconds, but there was no one in the room.

She could faintly hear the band playing her favorite Shakira song downstairs at the ball. Zora shimmied in celebration as she tiptoed to Ingrid's desk. The Book of Risas was right there. She had hoped Ingrid hadn't taken it along, like she always did to record something funny she saw or when the muse of humor struck.

At first, Zora had been tempted to replace the interior of the Book of Risas with bad poetry, or even better, something in technical English like a computer manual, but she didn't have time to plan it.

Instead, she and Skylar had agreed on a better course of action. One that would be riskier but had the potential to stop this war of the first daughters and crown the Williams girls as the victors.

She sat in front of the computer and typed. Predictably, the computer's password was Risas.

Zora searched through files until she found the folder right there on the desktop. It contained all the addresses of the Lópezes's friends in Washington. The notes in the folder were a combination of holiday and goodbye/keep-in-touch cards.

Silly López girls!

Zora chuckled, imagining the looks of surprise on their friends' faces when they realized the cards contained embarrassing jokes from the Book of Risas!

The file share was connected to the Calligraphy Office. When Zora had pelted him with questions, Leo had explained that usually the department downloaded the messages the girls uploaded in the cloud, printed out the cards, and sent them to the girls' friends.

Just when she was settling down to finding the funniest joke in Ingrid's book to add as the last message these friends would get from the White House, the sound of footsteps startled her. She was afraid that even though she was dressed all in black, anyone could see her sitting by a desk and a computer that weren't hers, in a room she had no business being in.

For the first time, her conscience prickled her heart, but

hadn't Winnie said that this pranking was all in the spirit of having fun? Zora and Skylar had just followed along.

Whoever was patrolling the hallways continued along the main corridor. Zora glanced down at the Book of Risas and hurried to type a mash-up of jokes she found on the very first page. She snorted at the silly knock-knock jokes.

Knock, knock.
Who's there?
Water.
Water who?
Water you so excited about?

From the yellowing pages, she guessed this must not be Ingrid's most recent Book of Risas. The jokes inside were dreadful.

Knock, knock.
Who's there?
Candice.
Candice who?
Candice joke get any worse?

Zora was sure Leo or someone in Calligraphy would flag these messages.

She had to find something else. She deleted the jokes

she'd just typed and flipped through the notebook until she found a poem on the last page of Ingrid's journal.

"Eureka!" Zora said, and quickly typed.

Dear America, beautiful from coast to coast. But I . . .

Zora logged off the computer and tiptoed back to the closet. She was thrilled that this room would be hers once the López family moved out. She already had great plans for it.

She laughed all the way to the ball, and before dashing to the cloakroom, she peeked out from behind a giant tree decorated with electrical snowflakes. She saw her sister dressed as her, a total look of panic on her face that wouldn't belong on Zora ever. Would it?

Quickly she ran to the cloakroom and changed into Skylar's dress, stashing her spy outfit inside the backpack. She'd be back for it later. It was too good a disguise to lose.

Skylar's dress was a little too tight across Zora's chest, so she had to fight and make some unexpected contortions to zip it all the way up. She could hardly draw a breath. When she looked at her image in the mirror, she practiced Skylar's princess smile and wave. Although the gestures weren't perfect, they were close enough to help her pass as extrovert supreme Skylar.

Zora ventured into the ball, trying to glide across the

floor just like her sister would.

She passed her parents, who were dancing to a slow song as the ball wound down. Her dad caught her eye and winked at her. Zora tried to wink like Skylar would, but she only managed to blink fast with both eyes. Before her dad discovered what was up, Zora hurried away to join her sister.

She could tell Skylar's anxiety was increasing by the second. Zora cleared her throat so that it would hit the high pitch of Sky's enthusiasm and said, "Group photo?"

Skylar swirled around, and Zora had a surreal experience.

What was Skylar thinking as she saw herself in the gorgeous organza dress, smiling daintily and adorably, hopefully?

"Skylar!" Agent Lee exclaimed. Zora dressed as Skylar stood next to Agent Lee, beaming.

Javi, an expression of victory on his face, called Winnie from her spot by the tree, and the four girls lined up for the group picture.

Zora dressed as Skylar kissed Skylar dressed as Zora on the cheek and said, "You look majestic, sis."

And Skylar rolled her eyes and said, "Frivolities!"

The twins burst into laughter.

WINNIE

Winnie woke up the next day safe in the embrace of her many comforters and green-stained pillows.

She sat up and ran to the door to see if Laffy had come back for the bacon treats she'd left outside her room, in case her love wasn't enough.

"Whoa!" Michel, one of the Secret Service agents, exclaimed from his seat at the end of the hallway. "Everything okay, Win?" He put the newspaper down.

She shook her head, and he stood up so quickly his chair toppled back and the newspaper pages floated to the floor.

"Sorry, Mich," she said, helping him pick up the paper. "No sign of Laffy?"

He put the chair back and grimaced. "Sorry to say we haven't seen any traces of him." He smiled and added, "But on the bright side, no one tried breaking into your room or your sister's, either. Did you sleep well?"

She nodded, and her heart expanded with gratitude that Agent Sisco had kept his promise of watching her door. "I just wish Laffy would show up already," she said.

"He will. Have faith."

She waved at him and went back to her room. Dramatically, she flopped on her bed and exclaimed, "Where are you, Laffy?" The absence of her ferret felt like part of her heart was missing. The room was so lonely without him.

She texted Ingrid.

Are you okay? Any news?

Ingrid, who was an earlier riser than Winnie, didn't text back.

Instead, she barged into Winnie's room already dressed for the day.

"No news of the ferret," Ingrid said.

Winnie shook her head. Last night she had sat by that tree like she was one more decoration, hoping that once the guests left, Laffy would miss her at least a fraction of how much she missed him. But nothing would make him budge.

"Did you get the box with the glitter bomb back?" Winnie asked.

Ingrid sighed. "A guy from the Executive Building insisted the box was addressed to him, because his last name is Williams, too."

Winnie sat bolt upright on the bed. "What? But you got it, right?"

Ingrid shook her head. "Actually . . . . Sisco intervened."

Winnie clapped a hand to her forehead. "It exploded on poor Agent Sisco?"

"No, thank goodness," Ingrid said, crossing herself. "That guardian angel of first daughters must be working full-time, because nothing happened."

"Where is it, then?"

"Agent Sisco thought it was one of the white elephant presents and put it underneath the Christmas tree with the soda pop decorations, the one in the Visitors' Foyer."

"I'll go get it then," Winnie said, pulling her workout clothes from her chest of drawers. "Come with me."

"I can't."

"Why?" Winnie replied. "What are you doing now?"

"I'm going with Mami to a puppet show."

"A puppet show?" Winnie asked.

"Yes, in the Library. It will be fun. See you later," Ingrid said, and left.

Winnie was so wound up with worry about the fate of the glitter bomb, there was no way she'd sit through a show.

"See you later, Mich," she said, eager to make sure the prank reached its target for once and for all.

But Agent Michel stood and said, "Wait up. I'm coming along."

Winnie was grateful he'd watched her door the night before, but now she wanted to lose him. She needed to get the box.

She was heading to the foyer when Michel got a message on his earpiece and said, "The other way, Win. There's a tour for the holiday decorator volunteers, and Agent Sisco doesn't want the first family around."

She rolled her eyes, but since there was no shaking her security detail, she might as well get her workout of the day done.

She burned her energy by challenging Michel to races around the Rose Garden, playing tennis with Santiago the butler, who was done with his shift, and then a basketball shootout with Martha and Ray, who were waiting for bread dough to rise.

On the way back to her room, she saw Sisco was stationed by the Visitors' Foyer.

Winnie knew there would be no bypassing him. She was stinky with sweat anyway, so she headed to the shower instead.

Meet me in the hallway, she texted Ingrid.

But Ingrid must still have been at the puppet show, or else the phone's battery had died, because she never showed up.

Winnie tiptoed out of her room and peeked around a corner. Agents Michel and Lee were talking by the service stairs. She took her chance and dashed to the first floor, sliding down the banister with such bad timing that she landed on her backside right in front of a group of people she recognized as the holiday volunteers.

"Are you okay?" Sally, the volunteer coordinator, asked, offering a hand.

Winnie winced and took her hand. But in that moment, she saw one of the security dogs sniffing the glitter bomb, the dog's tail pointed like an arrow.

"Oh no!" Winnie said with a desperate sigh.

In the background, Annie, one of the Williams family's aides, was walking by with a delicate snow-white dress in her hands. Right by the tree, Senator Demetria King was on her phone. Her words trailed off midsentence when she too noticed the dog pointing at the present.

Winnie knew what would happen.

The dog pressed his nose against the box and started tugging at the plastic tag attached to the red ribbon around it. The tag that, when pulled, would detonate the glitter.

"No!" Winnie yelled, running toward the dog.

The visitors looked at her in horror, and then they all ducked at the sound of the box popping. . . and the glitter cloud spreading all over the Foyer, sticking to every little surface for dear life.

In the two or three seconds of absolute silence that followed, Winnie pressed her eyes tightly closed. She counted to five, wishing that when she opened them again, she'd be just waking up for the day. A clean slate of possibility ahead of her, instead of the punishment she for sure had coming after this. But when she opened them, the disaster was all too real.

"Oh my goodness!" Senator King exclaimed. One of the Secret Service agents had thrown himself on her to protect her from the glitter.

"It's ruined!" Annie, the aide holding the dress, lamented.

Pandemonium broke out.

Winnie wished she could unsee the mess in front of her. It was worse than a nightmare. The box had been so small, but glitter seemed to cover every surface. This was going to take forever to clean up. And she wasn't thinking only of the glitter.

The Secret Service agents were ushering the scared volunteers to a containment room.

"We need to make sure everyone's okay," Agent Michel said, but the men and women lining up looked very scared. Winnie felt really guilty.

"I'm sorry," she said, although no one seemed to hear her. Annie was crying like it was the end of the world.

But there was one sight that was the worst.

The poor dog was pawing at his nose as if it hurt, and Winnie's heart shattered.

She looked up at the stairs and saw Ingrid shaking her head in horror. The Williams sisters were there too, but they didn't look mad at Winnie, just scared for the dog.

The dog handler took him away without giving Winnie the chance to apologize.

Senator King advanced on Winnie, shaking a finger and hissing, "Young lady! You have disrespected the office of the president! Wait until your father finds out."

Whoops. Someone had heard her apology-slash-concession of guilt, all right.

As if he'd been summoned, the voice that made grown men shake exclaimed, "Winifred Esperanza López!"

Winnie's world spun. During her father's years in the presidency, she'd seen TV clips of him when something bad happened and the country wouldn't come together. He'd never used that voice at home, or with her.

"Up to the Solarium, now," he said. "You too, Ingrid."

In that moment, Mrs. Williams looked down from a balustrade, and in a voice as presidential as Papi's, she added, "Zora and Skylar, you heard the president. Solarium. Now."

Without being told twice, the girls scuttled to face their punishments.

The girls sat on a window bench. The sun was delicious on Winnie's back, the only comfort compared to the icy glare coming from the two sets of parents in front of her.

Ingrid pressed Winnie's hand in a comforting gesture, and Mami snapped, "Ingrid, please don't act like we asked impossible things of you. I mean, Winnie has always been impulsive, but never so thoughtless. And you? Why didn't you talk some reason into your sister's head? What have I told you about the significance of—"

"Two Latina girls and two Black girls living in the White House. Haters gonna hate and make racist comments," Ingrid recited.

Winnie wished she could disappear through the cracks in the hardwood floor. If Mami found out about the rest of the casualties of the prank war, she'd be terribly upset.

President-Elect Williams picked up just where Mami had stopped, as if they'd coordinated their telling-off. "And you two? We're still guests here at the White House, girls. Is this how you show your good upbringing?"

"We didn't think you'd need a babysitter, but I believe we'll need to ask Aunt Rita to come and stay with us," Mr. Williams added, disappointed.

"Not Aunt Rita!" Skylar and Zora exclaimed in unison.

The look of dismay on their faces was heartbreaking. Aunt Rita must be to them what Abuela Leti, Papi's mom, was for the Lópezes. Winnie and Ingrid had had a string of nannies over the years, and when their behavior didn't improve, Papi had warned that he'd call his mother, who had been strict enough to raise the first Latino president of the country.

The threat was usually enough for Ingrid and Winnie to shape up.

"If you four can't get along, we'll need some other kind of arrangement. We can move to a nearby hotel. Matías, I'm sorry about all this," the president-elect added. "That poor security dog and his handler . . . and Senator King!"

Senator King. The name alone conjured terror.

"I told her you'll be contacting her for some kind of community service to make up for the mess the glitter made, Winnie," Mami said.

Winnie placed her head in her hands. What kind of torture would Senator King devise to make her pay for what she'd done?

Mr. Williams added, "Annie was in hysterics over your dress, Skylar. Which, by the way . . . why did you go behind your mom's back to order a new one for the inauguration when you already had one that coordinates with Zora's?"

"You did?" Zora asked, dismayed. "I thought we were set . . ."

Skylar's cheeks flared such a brilliant red that Winnie's cheeks hurt in sympathy.

"I'm sorry!" Skylar's chin quivered and her voice wavered, but she didn't cry. "I wanted a completely different dress from yours." She took a shuddering breath and said, "This is all my fault!"

"No, it's *my* fault," Winnie said. "The glitter bomb was my idea."

"What were you thinking, Win?" Mami exclaimed.

Another uncomfortable silence fell on them.

"You have nothing to say for yourself?" Papi asked.

"I plead the Fifth," Winnie said, and mimicked zipping her lips. When she realized what she'd just said, she ducked, as if she wanted to hide inside a shell like a turtle.

Yes, she had been disobedient and reckless. But as the Fifth Amendment stated, it was her constitutional right to remain silent so she wouldn't get into even more trouble.

She was sure everyone was staring at her, and she lifted her eyes tentatively to see Ingrid, Zora, and Skylar pressing their lips together super hard, as if they were trying not to laugh.

But Papi shook his head and said, "This isn't funny, girls. This time the joke went too far." His voice was soft, but it cut Winnie to her core.

Agents Michel, Lee, and Sisco stood against a wall at attention. They didn't look at Winnie, but she knew they were aware of her every reaction. They wouldn't judge her or tell her off, but she felt like she had let them down.

She *had* let them down.

Duty to the country was always the first thing for every member of the staff. Winnie wished she had remembered their excellent example of always putting the honor of the house and the office of her job as first daughter in number one place.

When the atmosphere turned unbearably heavy, Zora spoke up. "It's my fault too. I was the mastermind of a few things I'm not particularly proud of. . . ."

She didn't elaborate, but at least she hadn't blamed Winnie and Ingrid to make her sister and herself look better.

"I'm sorry for everything," Winnie said.

"I'm sorry," the other girls echoed.

The grown-ups nodded.

"Winnie and Ingrid, to your rooms. Leave your phones here." Mami stood with arms crossed at the door.

"But . . . I need to text Javi to see if he wants to come over later," Winnie complained. "For the interview."

"Javi can talk to me first," Papi said. "That way he can get a clear picture of who you are."

Winnie was appalled that Papi would say this in front of the Williamses, as if he didn't trust her. "Really, Papi?"

The president nodded, his arms crossed and his forehead creased with disappointment.

"See you at dinner?" Ingrid asked the Williams sisters as she walked past them.

Mami tsk-tsked. "During dinner you can write letters of apology to the whole household," she said.

"Great idea," Mrs. Williams added.

Winnie dropped her head and took the punishment with dignity. It was the least she could do.

18

ZORA

January 20, Inauguration Day

Zora had watched countless hours of video and read countless books about presidential inaugurations. But like everything having to do with life at the White House, nothing could prepare her for the whirlwind of activity and emotions about to barrel over her and her family like a tidal wave.

The day they had moved to the White House, every memory had blurred together in a kaleidoscope of colors and images. She intended to remember every second of today so she could tell her descendants when she was an old lady.

Aunt Rita, Grandma Iris, and the whole family had come

into town for the history-making day, which for the Williams clan had started when the stars still shone in the sky.

"I wish we could be with Mom right now," Skylar said on the ride to the Capitol Building, where the inauguration would take place. "What must she be feeling?"

Aunt Rita, Mom's oldest sister, fixed her hat and said, "She's probably happy beyond measure. She's been dreaming about this day since she was a little girl, younger than you two."

Grandma Iris smiled. "The only two other times I've seen her so elated were when she and your daddy got married and when you girls were born."

"She was happier that day," Aunt Rita said.

"Yes, she was," said Grandma Iris.

Zora and Skylar smiled at each other, and a warmth spread in Zora's chest.

"Wave at the people," Grandma Iris said, lifting a gloved hand at the window.

Zora was about to say the people couldn't see them through the tinted windows, but when she turned her gaze, she gasped.

There were throngs of people. More than she'd ever seen in her life.

"The news said they started lining up last night," Grandma Iris said with pride in her voice.

The weight of what it really meant to be a first daughter hit Zora with force.

She wondered what Winnie and Ingrid were thinking in the car driving behind theirs in the cavalcade. As Javi had told her and Skylar at the Christmas ball, the change back to civilian life would be hard for the López girls. Yes, even Winnie, who kept saying she couldn't wait for her father's second term to end.

"Did you all ever find that rat?" Aunt Rita asked.

Skylar laughed. "Rat? It was a ferret!"

"Rodents," said Aunt Rita, shuddering. "I hope you get a dog if you get a pet."

Zora opened her mouth to corrent Aunt Rita. Ferrets were not rodents. But Skylar shook her head for her to let it go.

"Poor Laffy. He's so cute," Skylar said, peering out the window as if she hoped to see him waving a flag with the rest of the people. "Up until yesterday there were rumors he'd been seen frolicking outside."

"I hope not! It's been so cold," Zora said, her heart hurting for the ferret that had never been an outdoor pet.

The car slowed down, and Grandma Iris exclaimed, "We're here! We're going to freeze!"

Grandma was always so very practical and no-nonsense.

"I did my research, and there will be heaters above us

and in front of us," Zora said. "Don't worry, Grandma." She followed her family out of the car, and people clapped from behind the crowd-control barriers.

Zora and Skylar waved at them, and a cheer rose.

Grandma Iris and Aunt Rita waved back and followed Agent Lee to their assigned seats.

"Thanks for nagging me to wear a woolen coat, Sky," Zora said. "Yours looks fabulous."

Skylar beamed at her.

Zora hoped that the whole world could see that even if they shared the same DNA and looked identical, she and Skylar were two separate girls with separate dreams and hopes.

Zora and Skylar sat behind their parents, in the second row. The sun shone brightly, making the morning as perfect as anyone could ever have expected. Winnie, Ingrid, and the López family sat on the other section of the stage. Their faces were glowing as they celebrated one of their own for having completed his duty with honor.

Mom's leather-gloved hands were clasped as if in prayer. But when it was time for her to take the oath of office, there was no weakness or hesitation in her voice as she placed her hand on the Lincoln Bible that Dad held, and she recited, "I do solemnly swear that I will faithfully execute the office of President of the United States, and will, to the best of my ability, preserve, protect, and defend the Constitution of the United States."

There were a few seconds in which her words still rang out from the speakers placed all over the National Mall and beyond. The clamor of cheers rose like the sound of a wave. Everyone on the stage remained on their feet, clapping and cheering for the new president of the United States.

"I thought this day would never arrive, and now my little Theresa is the president!" Aunt Rita said, hugging Zora and Grandma Iris. Skylar reached out her hand and pressed Zora's. "She did it!" she said.

Suddenly, her face and Skylar's were on the huge screens posted at the sides of the stage, and the crowd roared in approval again. Skylar and Zora waved.

She looked over her shoulder and saw Javi next to his dad. He winked at her. She wondered what he'd written in the article that *Verified Teen* was publishing today.

But she didn't have time to think about the article anymore. It was time for Mom's inaugural address, her first words as president of the United States of America.

Dad went back to his seat, and Mom fleetingly locked eyes with Zora and Skylar, as if she was gathering strength for the next step.

Zora mouthed, "You're the best mom in the world."

Next to her, Skylar said, "I love you, Mom."

Mom—President Williams now, after the oath—blinked rapidly, and for a second Zora was afraid she'd made her cry. That hadn't been her intention.

But her mom was the strongest woman in the world. She squared her shoulders, took a last look at her family, and turned back toward the podium.

The millions of people gathered at the National Mall roared in excitement. President Williams tried to speak, but something in the way she set her shoulders told Zora her mom was perplexed about something.

Zora's hands prickled with nerves, sensing something was wrong. Very wrong.

"Dear America, beautiful from coast to coast . . . But I . . ."

Her voice was barely audible above the love from the crowd. The president stopped talking, and she turned around to look at now-former President López, who was whispering to Alice, their faces creased with alarm.

Zora knew for a fact that the speech her mom had prepared had a different opening line. True, her mom had changed it many times, adding or cutting a phrase here or there, but those words sounded like . . . like the poem Zora had typed up from Ingrid's journal and sent off to the Calligraphy Office! Although the temperature was frigid in Washington, DC, Zora's face burned.

What had she done?

Had she sent the file share to the wrong place?

After the glitter-bomb disaster, she and Skylar had run to the Calligraphy Office to stop Leo from printing the poem on the López girls' goodbye cards. But Leo had been baffled. He couldn't find the file, and soon enough Zora had thought there must have been a guardian angel of communications that had prevented the prank from going through.

She hadn't thought things would get crossed in the changing systems. Did her prank land on her mom's speech?

At that moment, there was a terrible sound of feedback, and the technicians got to work to fix it.

President Williams looked relieved at the chance to recover, but she still seemed worried. What was happening? Mom had to have memorized her speech, but President López had warned her that the stress of the moment could leave your mind blank, and to be ready with a script on the teleprompter.

Skylar seemed to come to the same realization in that split second. Sensing the heaviness on the stage, which had nothing to do with how many people were sitting there, Winnie and Ingrid leaned from the other section of seats and looked as if they were asking them what was going on.

Breaking protocol, Ingrid and Winnie left their seats and rushed toward Skylar and Zora, breathless.

Aunt Rita and Grandma Iris were shocked into silence

when they heard Ingrid's next words.

"That's from my dad's high school journal!" Ingrid said, looking at Zora and Skylar. "It was on my desk because I've been reading it all year."

Skylar snapped out of her horror first. "There's no time to explain! Once the microphones come back, my mom's going to read the wrong speech!"

"What have you done?" Winnie and Ingrid exclaimed in unison.

"We wanted to prank your goodbye cards, but instead we hijacked Mom's speech!" Zora confessed behind her hand, trying to keep a smile on her face because the cameras were always rolling.

This was a historic moment, and they had ruined it for everyone!

But instead of arguing, Winnie wove through the crowd on the stage with the confidence of a gymnast about to perform a triple-double jump and came back with Alice Sung's phone.

"It's connected to the teleprompter. Quickly!"

She passed it to Ingrid, who scanned the speech and deleted the poetry section.

Just in time too, because the crowds had silenced enough to allow the president to speak, and the microphones were working again.

The president started her speech. She hesitated for a

second, as if making sure everything was as it should be, and then she dived right into the words she'd crafted carefully for the nation. For those who'd voted for her and those who hadn't, all her people, one America.

Zora's eyes prickled with emotion. That she was privileged enough to sit on this stage and witness this moment! A historic moment for the world and her family.

A tiny nose peeked out from inside the podium, and at first Zora thought that it was her imagination, or that her vision was distorted from the tears flooding her eyes. But at the sound of Winnie's gasp, she knew she wasn't imagining things.

It was First Ferret Lafayette, lurking next to the president's feet. Had he really been outside all this time, then? If anyone startled him, he'd run over President Williams's feet, and she would scream. She wouldn't be able to stop her reaction.

Winnie made a sound of dismay, but in that instant, Agent Sisco bent down as if to pick up a piece of paper, and in a swift move, he grabbed the ferret and put him inside his coat.

He spoke into his earpiece and headed to the back of the stage.

SKYLAR

Agent Sisco didn't look too happy when the girls swarmed him after the inauguration, demanding the return of Laffy. The ferret was in the agent's arms, snuggled inside a blanket with the Secret Service five-pointed-star logo, soundly sleeping as if he'd had enough adventures to last him a lifetime.

Skylar felt bad for Agent Sisco, and her heart softened. She'd been so nervous around this man of such stern expression, and now she could see beyond the unreadable features. He was committed to his job. Most important, he truly loved the first family, and the López family loved him back.

"If I give him to you now, he could run away again. We'd lose him for sure!" he exclaimed between clenched teeth, glancing behind the girls as if he expected a last-minute threat on the first family just when he could taste the freedom at the end of his assignment.

"Please," said Winnie. "His cage is being packed right now, and I want him to have the chance to be home one last time."

"Winnie," he said, and he sounded like he was trying, really trying, not to roll his eyes, "I can't—"

Winnie placed a hand on his shoulder, and Skylar saw him relax under her touch. "I know we've been a pain, but trust us. I promise that nothing will happen."

His shoulders slumped. Laffy squirmed in his arms and opened one eye as if the ferret had been pretending to be asleep all this time but in truth had been listening in on their conversation.

"Okay," he said. "But girls, please, no more escapades or glitter or ferret ice cubes or anything else. I beg you."

Winnie stood on her tiptoes and kissed Agent Sisco on the cheek. It was the first time Skylar had seen him completely disarmed. Without a word, just a little tilt of the corners of his mouth that could pass as a smile, the agent passed the snoozing pest formerly known as First Ferret Lafayette into the hands of former First Daughter Winnie.

227

Skylar would never get a ferret. She wasn't even sure she and her sister would get a pet, so Laffy's reputation as the first ferret of the nation would continue indefinitely.

"I'll come to the house with you," Zora said to Winnie. "Agent Lee can drive us."

When they were off, Skylar was happy that her sister had decided to do so without looking to her for approval.

Already things were different. But they felt good.

While everyone was dispersing for photos at the White House and to get ready for the inaugural balls, Skylar turned to Ingrid and said, "Do you want to help me choose some jewelry for tonight?"

Ingrid clapped in excitement, and they chattered all the way to her room, where Ingrid helped Skylar pick a tiara that had tiny points like cat ears. "That'll go perfectly with your new dress."

Skylar glanced at her dress hanging from a rack and bit her lip with excitement. "I still can't believe we all got these loaner dresses for tonight. It's like a dream!"

"It did turn out better than if we'd planned it," Ingrid said.

Rhea peeked inside the room and lit up at the sight of Ingrid. "Ingrid, your sister needs help with her hair."

Ingrid smiled knowingly. "I'll be right there," she said, and nodded at Skylar.

"Thanks for your advice!"

"Of course! See you tonight at the ball."

Skylar placed the tiara on her head and beamed at her reflection in the mirror. She was the luckiest girl in the country, going to the most exclusive party in town. She was excited to share the night with her three best friends: her sister, and Ingrid and Winnie.

Her parents would have to stop by at least eight different parties thrown in their honor, but the girls would get to stay all night long with the teens and kids of politicians here at the official inaugural ball at the White House.

When the four girls went down the majestic stairs, every eye was on them.

Were people wondering if they hated each other? Were they all waiting for one last joke? Well, the joke was on them, because all the newspapers and news sites got were shots and clips of Zora and Winnie in a dance-off for the ages.

Skylar hadn't seen Javi's piece for *Verified Teen* yet, but as she clapped and cheered for the two dancing girls in the center of the room, she hoped he'd captured how special the friendship that bound the first daughters was.

"Your turn!" Winnie exclaimed, pointing at Skylar, who was thrilled that this time she didn't have to run from room to room pretending to be someone else. Tonight, she was completely herself, in her first pair of high heels, and she loved it.

Although the party ended well into the morning, the celebrations and recognitions were not over. Winnie and Ingrid had invited Skylar and Zora to Agent Sisco's retirement breakfast.

Agent Steve Sisco's parents beamed with pride as now-former President López shook his hand and the whole room rose to its feet and cheered for him, a true national hero. Being in the first row, Skylar clearly read Mr. López's lips when he leaned in to Sisco and said, "I might still pull some strings for a medal of honor for making sure Popcorn and Parakeet didn't get into too much trouble."

The whole room was clapping. They hadn't heard these last words, but the López girls clapped louder than anyone and cheered for their hero and friend, who looked happy and grateful—grateful that the job was over and he could now take a nap in peace.

After breakfast came the hardest moment of all.

The four girls had grown so close during the last seven weeks of sharing the executive mansion. Even in the moments when it seemed to Skylar that they hated each other—maybe even especially during these moments. But in the end, they knew the time to part ways would come, and no one was ready. Skylar had heard Mrs. López say goodbye to the staff the morning of the inauguration, before heading out. She'd broken into tears of gratitude for the people who'd become a family to her, her daughters, and the president.

She'd joked about how she wouldn't survive her mornings without her made-to-order cafecito and croissants, but Skylar knew it was more than that making her cry. And now the girls stood in a little circle, in a group hug of first daughters, because there were no words that could describe what they were feeling.

Winnie, eager to see the world and make a name for herself.

Ingrid, afraid of feeling lonely, but at the same time, excited for the friends she would meet.

Zora, ready to discover the secrets of the house and to leave her mark on history. She was already doing so.

And Skylar, knowing that she was loved for who she was and not for who her family was.

Agent Lee gave them a moment of privacy, but then it was time to go.

Zora and Skylar stood on the North Lawn waving goodbye to their friends. They watched them get into the black SUVs.

Then Zora looked at Skylar and said, "Ready to go into our new rooms?"

Skylar's heart pretty much jumped out of her mouth. This was it. She and Zora were officially the first daughters, and a voice inside her told her that she was ready to do the First Kids Club proud.

They raced each other to the second floor, where they'd been mostly as spies, when they'd snuck into the López girls' rooms. Skylar was in awe of the change in the decorations already. The portraits on the wall and the personal touches were all hers and her sister's.

When she walked into her perfect room and saw a package on the bed, she gasped.

"Zora!" she called. "Come here!"

Zora zoomed into Skylar's room and skidded to a stop. The box on the bed looked suspiciously like the package where Ingrid and Winnie had hidden the glitter bomb that had coated the Visitors' Foyer in glitter. Off-white with an innocent-looking tag hanging from a ribbon.

Perfect. Lethal. Destructive.

They looked at each other through narrowed eyes.

"Seriously?" asked Skylar. "After all the apologizing and hugging?" A part of her felt wounded that the López girls would spring another last-second prank just to have the final word.

But Zora was the optimist and the adventurous one. "I'll open it. In case it's another glitter bomb, I'll take the responsibility."

Skylar wasn't eager to get glitter-bombed, but she wasn't going to let her sister take the risk by herself. "We'll open it together," she said.

The night before the big move, Mom had been right, as always. In order to feel loved and cherished, first one must love and cherish those around them.

Zora seemed pleasantly surprised. "Okay, on the count of three."

They looked at each other and counted, "One, two, three."

They pulled on the tag, and the box fell apart, showing three things: a copy of *Verified Teen* that still smelled of fresh ink, a framed photo of the four first daughters at the inaugural ball dancing their feet off like fairy-tale princesses, and a letter.

Skylar felt a knot in her throat.

She looked up, and Zora had tears in her eyes too.

She picked up the heavy cream-colored paper with the López sisters' initials. She handed it to Ingrid. "Read it," she said softly.

Zora cleared her throat and read,

Dear Zora and Skylar,

Surprise! It's not another glitter bomb. We bet you were nervous, ha! We didn't want to pass up this opportunity to write a welcome letter to you both.

Welcome to the First Kids Club!

There are so many rules and limitations in this job none of us chose for ourselves, but there are also so many amazing things. Although we're excited for the next step in our lives, we're also sad that our sweet time here is ending.

Your experience will be similar to ours, but at the same time, it will be really different! First of all, we were so young when our dad became the president that we don't know anything else. We grew up surrounded by loads of people who loved us and protected us that we don't know how we will adapt to being a family of only four! But your teenage years are barely starting, and you'll have to navigate situations we were spared (or missed out on, depending on how you see it). Like having your first kiss (we heard the roof is very private for this) or going to your first school dance. (The Secret Service will come along too. No getting out of it!)

Two Latina girls growing up at the White House was a sacrilege to some people, and they won't be any happier to see two confident, beautiful, smart Black girls either. Don't waste energy on the haters.

We don't have a lot of advice, except to tell you to enjoy every second. Know that no matter what the news or the polls say, at the end of the day, our parents are still just humans who have devoted their lives to the service of others. Remember who your mom really is! No matter what the haters say about the president or your family.

The lessons you'll learn just by living in the White House with your parents will be more valuable than any you could learn in the classroom. Like you saw on the campaign trail, this country of ours is a beautiful place built on the foundation of the sacrifice of the people before us. There's still lots of work to do, but we have come so far!

We love the United States, the people we've met, and especially you, dear friends. Reach out anytime, especially when you need to vent. Nobody else knows what it's like to be the first daughters like we do!

With love from your friends,
Winnie and Ingrid López
P.S. See you tomorrow on the video call!

Zora and Skylar looked at each other and hugged.

"Are you ready to go over Javi's article?" asked Zora.

Skylar beamed at her, and together, they skimmed through Javi's write-up of the first daughters. It was the first time she'd ever seen so much melanin on the cover of *Verified Teen*. The article highlighted how the four girls had supported each other as they transitioned into and out of the White House.

"These photos from the Christmas ball are beautiful!" Zora said. "Look at your face when you were pretending to be me!"

They laughed at the strained expression on Skylar's face.

"But the ones you sent him from when we were little are the best," Skylar said, resting her head on Zora's shoulder.

They both gazed at the images that marked important events in their lives. Always together. Since the very beginning.

"I'm glad you're my twin," Skylar said. "And I think now is time to celebrate."

"Celebrate what?" Ingrid asked.

"That we're in the First Kids Club. It sounds fun, huh?"

"It sounds awesome," said Ingrid, and they hooked their arms and headed to the kitchen to exercise one of their privileges: strawberry parfaits!

INGRID

Ingrid looked at the White House with longing. Her one true home. Next time she was here, she'd be a guest, and although a part of her mourned the loss of this time in her life, another was excited for what would come next.

She guessed the rest of her family had similar feelings.

Her dad got into the front passenger side just as the last moving van was closing up and pulling out of the driveway. Toward the future. The furniture and stuff would drive ahead to California, but the family would stop at their leisure throughout the country.

Their first time as civilians in eight years. They still had security, but it wasn't as restrictive as before.

Mami dabbed the corner of her eye with one of the

handkerchiefs Abuela Rebecca had made especially for this occasion. They'd been sprayed with anti-sadness lavender and chamomile, and either it was not working or the tears in Mami's eyes were a combination of feelings that went way beyond sadness.

Finally the driver put the car into gear and their SUV started down the driveway.

As the White House fell away behind them, Papi turned around and looked at the girls and Mami, who smiled back at him.

"What?" asked Winnie, guessing that he had something to say.

He chuckled, his cheeks bright red, his eyes sparkling. He looked at Mami, and the two of them started laughing. The girls looked at each other in alarm.

Finally Papi said, "You two and your prank war!"

"Thank goodness Winnie thought quickly and was able to fix the speech!" Mami said, fanning herself.

They all joined in laughter, even the driver.

"How did you know?" Winnie asked.

Mami smiled her Mona Lisa smile and said, "Remember, I know everything. That's a power I'm not losing in the move, so you two better watch out!"

Ingrid winced.

"I'm glad you girls could figure out how to work through your differences," Papi added. "Sometimes politics can feel like a war of pranks too, but in the end, it's important to remember what comes first. It's better to have friends than to be right. Cierto, Winnie?"

Winnie nodded.

Ingrid sniffed, and she hoped it was a leftover from the tears and not because she was getting a cold. She put her hand inside her pocket and felt a piece of paper. She opened it up and saw a note that read:

Here's the website for the California School of Comedy Summer Camp.
Good luck!
First Gentleman Beau Williams

A warmth spread through Ingrid's chest. She couldn't wait to meet all the friends she'd make at camp. She couldn't wait to tell Zora, Skylar, and Javi all about it.

A dooking sound coming from the carrier secured in the middle seat called Ingrid's attention. Laffy closed his eyes, enjoying the air coming in through the open window. Winnie had a smile on her face as the wind made her long brown hair flutter. Free.

Ingrid savored the moment.

"Knock, knock," she said.

"Who's there?" replied the rest of the family in unison as the car drove down the road.

ACKNOWLEDGMENTS

This book was a blast to write, and it wouldn't exist without the work of a team of brilliant professionals who share the same passion as mine: a love of story. My editors Claudia Gabel and Stephanie Guerdan, thank you for all your amazing guidance and feedback! Working with you has been an honor. Thank you also to the rest of the HarperCollins family: Laaren Brown, Renée Cafiero, Chris Kwon, Kristen Eckhardt, Emily Zhu, and Lauren Levite. And thank you to Nia Davenport for your feedback and expertise!

Kat Fajardo, thank you for the amazing cover. I've admired your art for a long time and I'm thrilled we crossed paths on this project.

My agent, Linda Camacho, my fairy godmother, thanks for making all my dreams come true. I'm the luckiest author! Thank you also to Marietta Zacker and the rest of the Gallt and Zacker family.

Thank you to my friends: Veeda Bybee, for believing in me and my words, and reminding me of all the light and good in the world when things turned very hard and very dark. You were the first person to meet the first daughter squad, and your love for it kept me going.

Thank you, Courtney, Juli, Karina, Anedia, and Alicia for being the best cheerleaders.

Ally, Lindsey, Renée, Rachel, Ash, Alex, and Desta: what a joy it was to work on this book during Allycon with you! Let's do it again soon!

Natalie Mickelson, Rachel Seegmiller, and Verónica Muñoz, without you, there would be no books. Thank you for your love and support.

Iris Valcárcel, you left this world while I was still revising this story, before I could tell you about my dreams for this new project, before the pandemic struck, way before I was ready for you to go, amiga querida. I miss you so much, but rest assured I'll never forget that you love me mucho mucho.

I'm so grateful to my writing community: Las Musas, VONA, VCFA, SCBWI, Storymakers, and WIFYR.

Thank you to my family scattered all over the world: Los Saied in all their iterations, the Méndez clan, and the friends who celebrate each of my triumphs because a victory for one is a victory for all.

Damián, María Belén, y Gonzalo, primos, primas, tíos, tías, los quiero mucho y les dedico todos mis libros con mucho amor.

Mami, siempre en mis recuerdos y mi corazón. Espero que desde el cielo veas el fruto de tu fe, amor, y esfuerzo y estés orgullosa de mí.

Ruby Cochran-Simms, dear English teacher and friend, thanks for giving me the tools of my craft. I don't know the words in English or Spanish to express the depth of my gratitude for the impact you've had in my life. Who would have imagined that a girl from el 7 de septiembre would one day be writing—in English! — about four girls and their adventures in the White House? And yet, here I am. Thank you for believing in me!

When I was nineteen years old, I moved to the United States with a small suitcase and a heart full of dreams, most of which have come true, at least the most important ones. I love Argentina, the land where I was born and raised, and I also love this country where I've grown deep roots. In all its beauty, greatness, and imperfections, I love the United States and its people. I'm honored at having the chance to write a story in which four girls of color live, love, play, and grow in the most famous residence in the world. Every child deserves to see themselves in a book that celebrates childhood and all its wonders.

Dear young reader, I never take for granted the great honor and responsibility of sharing my stories with you. Thank you for spending time with my characters and me. Thank you to the teachers, librarians, parents, and caregivers who foster a love for learning and books.

And last but never least, thank you to my husband, Jeff, our children, Julián, Magalí, Joaquín, Areli, and Valentino, and our pets, Dandelion, Nova, and Coraline. You fill my life with light and joy. Thank you for the one-liners and the endless inspiration. Los amo.